TROUBLE

BAD BOY HOMECOMING/B-SQUAD NOVELLA

AVERY FLYNN

ACKNOWLEDGMENTS

A huge thank you to Carrie Ann Ryan for organizing this Bad Boy Homecoming and for sending some of the best/weirdest texts ever. Also, it was a blast to work with Katee Robert (loved plotting the Jackson family with you), Stacey Kennedy (my new favorite person to Skype with), and Kennedy Layne (the caffeine from our shared coffee addiction could run the world). And I couldn't not say thank you to Charity Hendry for the gorgeous cover! Girl, you have SKILLS! As always, a big thank you to the Flynn family. I couldn't do anything without you. xoxo

Cover design by Charity Hendry (www.CharityHendry.com)
Edited by Nicole Bailey Proof Before You Publish
ISBN: 978-0-9964763-8-6 (Digital)
ISBN: 978-0-9964763-9-3 (Print)

1

Leah

I t was the boobs. It was *always* the boobs.

They weren't like the-plane's-going-down-emergency-flotation-device big, but they were large enough that Leah Camacho was used to idiots who never looked her in the eyes trying to buy *the girls* drinks—or, in this case, upgrade her compact rental to a luxury Aston Martin DB9.

"You're the one hundredth customer today," the guy behind the car rental counter said. "It's totally legit."

Leah looked around. The place was empty. It was ten in the morning. There was no signage saying anything about a luxury upgrade contest. Sarah—according to the guy's name tag—was the only one working. He had a thick mustache, shaggy blonde hair, and the company shirt he wore about three sizes too small, barely making the stretch across his broad chest. Her bullshit meter was off the charts. She glanced out the front door, ready to walk back out into the July Fort Worth heat—it wasn't a dry heat or a humid heat it was just an oppressive, thank-God-someone-invented-air-conditioning face-of-the-sun kind of heat—and Uber her way to another car rental place when the black sports car parked outside snagged her attention.

It was all sleek lines and badass beauty. She'd make the three-hour trip from Fort Worth to Catfish Creek in half the time. Of course, that may not be a plus. It's not like she was all that excited to return to her small hometown for her ten year high school reunion. If it wasn't for the opportunity to see the cute cheerleaders who'd made her life hell back then now looking like life had bitch slapped them around, she probably would have ignored the invite. Petty? Absolutely. However, anyone who said that wasn't at least part of their reasoning for attending a high school reunion when high school had been one of Dante's lower levels of hell was a big, fat liar. Anyway, there was no denying that this car would make a helluva better impression than a silver compact with zero pickup and a tinny horn. Plus, her best friend Gray would go ape shit. A mechanic and total gear head, he'd probably pet the damn thing and whisper sweet nothings into its intake manifold.

Decision made, Leah turned back to the man behind the counter who had developed a slick sheen of sweat on his forehead. Boyfriend here was nervous.

"And what do you want from me?" She dropped her gaze to his name tag. "Sarah?"

He shoved the printed contract across the counter to her along with a pen. "Just your signature."

"Same price?"

He nodded and pushed the paperwork another two inches toward her.

What the hell? If her boobs were gonna give her a back-ache and ruin her for strapless dresses unless she wore the mother-of-all-industrial-strength bras, she might as well get something out of them besides catcalls and unsubtle leering. She picked up the pen and signed.

Three minutes later her suitcase was in the tiny trunk, her purse on the passenger seat and she was behind the wheel, the rental contract still in her hand. Reaching across the dashboard, she popped open the glove box and pushed the paperwork inside. One corner didn't slide in easily. She patted her hand around inside and pulled out a small, hot pink satin bag with a cartoon unicorn stitched onto it. Something hard was in the bag. She tugged open the strings holding it closed and spilled out the contents into her palm. It was a diamond-shaped paperweight or kid's toy, she couldn't tell. Obviously, the last people who rented the Aston Martin before her had forgotten it. No doubt, some poor kid was seriously bummed out.

She turned the key in the ignition. Then, she pictured a little kid with her eyes all puffy from crying because her parents had forgotten the kid's prized possession. Damn. It sucked being let down by the people around you—no one knew that better than Leah. There was no way she could hit the road with some kid's fake diamond. She cut the engine.

Sighing, she got out of the car to turn in the bag so the rental people could contact the previous renters, but the building had gone dark. The open for business sign had been changed to Out For Lunch Back At with the little clock on the sign reading eleven thirty.

Great.

She got back in the car and tossed the bag back in the glove compartment and closed it. She'd remember to turn it in on Monday when she returned the car. Unable to delay the inevitable any longer, she turned the key in the engine and let the car purr for a minute before pulling out onto the road and heading to the one place in the world she'd sworn she'd never go back to--funny how fate just loved to laugh at declarations like that.

Drew

Catfish Creek

For the fifth time that week—and hopefully the last in his quickly dwindling tenure, Sheriff Drew Jackson knocked on Beauford Lynch's front door, standing off to the side just far enough that if the old goat let loose with his shotgun the blast would miss its target but not so far to the side that Beauford's wife, Betty Sue, would think Drew was being rude. The situation pretty much described life in Catfish Creek: smile and protect your balls.

The door opened, revealing Beauford in a pair of pressed jeans and a God Bless Texas T-shirt. The shotgun was nowhere to be seen. Some of the tension leaked out of Drew's shoulders.

"Morning, Mayor."

The other man crossed his arms and narrowed his eyes, taking in Drew's worn jeans and plain white T-shirt. With only a few days left as Catfish Creek's sheriff, since he lost the election, he'd become sheriff in name only—except, of course, for paying house calls on the mayor.

"Sheriff," Beauford said with a curt nod.

No shotgun, but no welcome either. Looked like it was

going to be one of those mornings. "Maisy Aucoin filed a complaint this morning, she says you've been harassing her cat."

"The damn thing keeps coming in my yard," Beauford sputtered. "Am I supposed to just welcome invaders with open arms?"

Drew managed not to laugh. It wasn't easy. The town's perpetual mayor for life was acting as if he was fighting terrorists or the East Coast liberal elite. "It's a tabby cat."

"It's my property," the other man shot back, an ugly red flush starting to climb its way north from his T-shirt collar.

"Does the cat destroy any of your property?"

"Not the point."

Drew sighed. This was ridiculous. God give him the patience to make it to five p.m. Friday, only four short days away. "Couldn't you just ignore the cat?"

The other man threw up his hands in frustration. "And *this* is why you lost the election."

"My even-handedness?" Drew asked, keeping his tone casual even as his heart rate sped up.

"Because you kowtow to people like Maisy Aucoin instead of listening to the folks who matter," the mayor said with a sneer. "We expected more of you considering your family name, which is why we appointed you to finish out Ned Finnigan's term after his heart attack."

"Mrs. Aucoin is the town librarian, she's not the criminal underbelly."

"She's a rebel rouser." Beauford's voice went up to a full shout on the last two words.

"Because she wouldn't get rid of the romance section of the library?"

"That trash doesn't need to be within sight of our young people," he huffed.

The man was delusional. "You mean the *young people* with full access to the *Internet*?"

The mayor jabbed a finger in Drew's direction. "Don't you backtalk me, boy."

In a normal place, being thirty-one would eliminate being called boy. Not in Catfish Creek, the town that sanity forgot. Not for the first time in the past two years, he wanted to kick himself for agreeing to come home in return for his mom agreeing to go to rehab. The kick wouldn't have changed anything, he'd have still come home, but it would at least have been an acknowledgement of the hell he was entering. Drew gave Beauford a tight smile and forced his right hand to unclench before he gave into the urge to punch a seventy-six-year-old man in the face.

"Maisy has agreed to keep her cat indoors during the day and to erect a barrier to the top of the fence between your yards. However, cats being cats, Mr. Darcy is bound to figure a way around the barrier. My request is that if that happens, you not blast the tabby into next week."

The red flush went all the way up to the roots of his white hair. "I have a right to protect my property."

"Beauford calm down before you have to take one of your pills." Betty Sue appeared next to her husband in the doorway, a yellow Tupperware that was probably older than Drew but still looked new in her hand. "I cut you a slice of my pecan pie and wrapped up some biscuits for you. Think of it as a parting thank you gift for your time as sheriff, although I hear you're only sheriff in name only, what with this being your last week."

Ignoring the half-insult because his mouth was watering in a sort of Pavlov's dog response, he reached out and accepted the container. "Thank you, ma'am."

Betty Sue gave him a big smile that said you're welcome

and I'm done with you two idiots at the same time. "Now, my program is about to start so I'm gonna help you two end this conversation. Beauford, you're not shooting at that cat anymore." She turned to Drew. "And you tell Maisy Aucoin that if her cat bothers my Catfish Creek County Fair-winning prized yellow roses again, I will light up the durned feline like the Alamo on the Fourth of July."

Knowing this was about as good as it was going to get in the war of neighbors, he tipped his hat. "Yes, ma'am."

Making his way back to his truck—his patrol car had already gone to Sheriff-elect Paul Airman—he popped the Tupperware lid and inhaled the heaven that was Betty Sue Lynch's homemade butter biscuits and secret recipe pecan pie. He had a biscuit halfway to his mouth when the screech of someone taking the corner at a high rate of speed tore through the quiet street, followed by a soft pop. Then, a black sports car that looked like something James Bond would drive flew past, sparks flying from the driver's side back wheel which had popped its tire somewhere along the line. Stuffing the biscuit in his mouth, Drew rushed to his truck, yanked open the door, tossed the Tupperware onto the passenger seat, grabbed the cherry top that suction cupped to the roof, and started the engine for pursuit. Adrenaline coursed through his veins, he pulled out and slammed his foot down on the gas. It was almost like being back on the force in Fort Worth.

But just his luck, the car jerked to a stop half a block down.

Spinning the wheel as he hit the brakes, he came to a stop behind the sports car at an angle that blocked it from reversing. Mrs. Yancy's huge Cottonwood tree cut off any forward motion. Drew got out of his truck, keeping the open door between him and the other car and flicked open the leather strap on his hip holster that kept his sheriff's office-issued 9mm locked in place.

"Get out of the vehicle," he hollered.

The car's driver's side door opened wide. The first part of the driver to appear was one shapely leg wearing skin-tight denim punctuated with scuffed up black Doc Martens. Some sort of danger alarm sounded in Drew's head, but not the kind that warned of bullets or other bodily danger. A woman got out, facing away from him, her hands up and her dark hair a long silky curtain that led his attention straight down her back to the high curve of her ass poured into those jeans. Parts of him that had no place in police business sat up and noticed. Her ass was a testament to the reason why society required women to wear full dresses for so long—because men were weak, lust-addled idiots when it came to asses like the one that looked more than a little familiar to Drew. His gaze snapped back up as his internal alarm went from quiet buzz to all-out blare. He *knew* that ass, that hair, and those damn boots.

"Turn around," he ordered.

She did. Her lush mouth—one he knew far too well—was compressed into a tight line, her attention focused on something behind him. Leah Camacho was back and with her always came trouble—for him, for his sanity, and for the part of him that still thought of her at opportune moments in the shower when his soapy hand was wrapped around his hard cock.

"Drew," she said, making his name sound like a curse and a promise. "Get on the other side of the door."

Listening to Leah Camacho was the last thing he should be doing, but he did it anyway for reasons he didn't understand. Just as he rounded the door, an extended cab pickup truck turned the corner. The tires were big, the windows dark, and the speed was slow. As it puttered by, Drew looked it over and mentally confirmed it didn't belong to any of the usual suspects in Catfish Creek. Of course, the high school reunion was bringing in lots of folks who hadn't been here in a while. At the corner, the truck sped up, peeling away from the stop sign and taking a hard right back toward the highway.

"Who was that?" he asked, the smell of burnt rubber drifting back toward them.

"No fucking clue but they've been on my ass for the past hour," she said, reaching up and winding her long hair into a knot on the top of her head—the move emphasizing her amazing tits and making Drew's mouth go dry. "When they pulled off the highway and followed me to Catfish Creek I listened to that little voice that said they were up to no good. I didn't realize I'd be stopping on your turf."

He bet not. After what happened last time they were together, she'd made avoiding him into an art form. The fact that even now half his brain was playing back dirty movies —the kind where she was spread out and naked before him or her red lips were wrapped around his dick or a close-up view of her slick, swollen pussy so hungry for his cock, his tongue or his fingers—showed just how much better it would be for him if she kept avoiding him. However, the fact that he was the law in town, however temporarily, meant avoiding her was an impossibility because wherever Leah Camacho went, trouble was sure to follow. He glanced down at exhibit A.

"What happened to your tire?" he asked.

"No clue," she said, her voice tight with a lie. "I must have run over something."

Drew squatted down and took a closer look at the tire. It didn't have a tear, it was just gone as if it had been a blow out. If Leah had run over something big enough to do that, she would have realized it.

"What in the hell is going on, Leah?"

Leah

If Leah had an answer to that question she'd be telling it to Drew as fast as she could, just so she could get the hell away from him before her panties combusted. Last she'd heard Drew was a cop in Fort Worth. What in the hell was he doing here with a sheriff's badge on a chain around his neck, a police light on his truck, and a few biscuit crumbs on the front of his white T-shirt? That little detail should have made him less hot. Sadly, it did not.

He must have caught her staring because he glanced down and brushed away the crumbs. She inhaled a deep breath and tried to force a moment of Zen to happen so she'd stop thinking about just what he liked to do with those strong hands when they were both naked, sweaty, and desperate for release. Of course, because she was trying to do the opposite that meant all she could picture was the wicked look on his face when he wrapped a silk tie around her ankle and secured one leg to the footboard before turning his attention to her other ankle.

And after?

Oh God.

After.

Her nipples tightened to hard buds as she ground her back molars together and did mental inventory of her most demanding customers' annoying quirks to banish the memory from her mind. It worked. Sort of. Well, at least enough for her brain to start forming words again.

"I thought you were in Fort Worth," she said, sounding almost like she wasn't about to jump his bones in the middle of Sam Houston Avenue.

"Not anymore. For the next few days I'm still the Catfish Creek Sheriff, but don't change the subject," he said in the low, rumbly thing his voice did when he was pissed. "What kind of trouble are you in now?"

Ah. Yes. She'd forgotten. She was back in Catfish Creek where nothing ever changed and people were always the same as they'd been the day they'd peaked—or plateaued— in high school. That meant that she couldn't possibly be anything other than the girl who dressed in all black and hung out with all the pot heads behind the football stadium and took advanced calc with the nerds. Never mind the fact that she owned one of the most successful marijuana shops in the state of Colorado, was on the board of her local small business association in Denver, and contributed to local charities because in Catfish Creek she'd always be Leah Camacho, bad girl with a big brain.

Decade-old resentment started to float to the surface and she planted a hand on one of her hips. "Why would I be in trouble?"

Drew raised an eyebrow and snorted. "You pull into town like a rocket in a fancy car that you're driving into the ground like money doesn't mean a thing to you."

"I own a successful business." Not successful enough for an Aston Martin in the garage, but what did she care?

"You run a pot shop," he retorted.

"Yeah, one that's totally legal in Denver." She should have expected the judgment she heard in Mr. By the Book's tone, but like an asshole, she hadn't. That stung. "Why, do you want to search the car?" Unable to stop herself from tormenting the both of them, she took a step closer to him and looked up at him through her thick eyelashes knowing just how much he liked to feel in charge—he never took that domineering attitude off, not even when he took off the badge. "You wanna search me?"

His body stiffened. "I don't think that's necessary."

For a second, she teetered on the edge of reaching out and touching him—letting her fingers skim down the length of his broad shoulders, across the solid wall of muscle he called a chest, and over the hard plane of abs in a journey that led straight to his belt buckle and all the hard goodness that was tucked away inside his pants—but she pulled back just in time, snapped out of the coquette imitation and back to her normal self. "Good, then how about helping me change the tire?"

He let out a half groan, half sigh and started to roll up his sleeves. "Give me the jack."

She could change the tire. It wasn't that she didn't know how, but some things were too good to miss. Seeing Drew Jackson's forearms flex as he went to work on her flat tire was one of them, especially when he'd be so focused on the job at hand that he wouldn't know she was watching.

"So what's the deal with those guys following you?" he said in mid-tire change.

Leah had noticed the ginormous truck in her rearview mirror about thirty miles outside of Fort Worth. It hadn't gotten weird until she noticed the truck mirroring every one of her moves as she switched lanes, passed cars and did an almost stop at a gas station. By the time she'd gotten to Catfish Creek, adrenaline was slingshotting through her body hitting every nerve.

"I really don't know." She wished like hell she was lying, but she had no frickin' clue who those assholes were.

Drew grunted in answer and finished putting on the donut tire he'd gotten out of the trunk. "This should get you to the service station. They'll probably have to order the tire you need. I doubt that Vasquez's Auto Care carries Aston Martin-approved tires."

Oh, she was so not forking over that kind of cash. "It's a rental."

"That's one way to treat yourself."

Pride pricked at his disapproving tone, she doubled down on his obvious belief that she was some sort of drug queen pin. "At least I know how to have a good time."

He stood up, eyeballing her from head to foot and back up again as he wiped his hands on the small mechanic's towel that had been in the trunk next to the jack. The look made her flush in all the best ways as warm desire slid across her skin as tangible as a lover's touch. Judging by the knowing smirk on his face, he noticed.

"As I recall," he said, tossing the towel in the small compartment where he'd already put the jack, "you know how to do a lot of things—most of which don't exactly fit in the good category."

Not when it came to them. "Are you flirting with me, Drew Jackson?"

His jaw tightened. "Of course not."

Bam. Direct hit. The quick way he'd answered in the negative was a solid smack to her ego—and picked the Drew-sized scab on her heart.

"It just wouldn't do for the sheriff to flirt with the big bad pot store owner in combat boots, now would it?" Their time together had only lasted for the summer after graduate school and had been totally covert, but it had been hot, intense and the marker by which she judged all affairs. Obviously, it hadn't had the same effect on perfect Drew Jackson, first-born son to one of the most powerful families in town and older brother to the bitchy queen bee of Catfish Creek High School who'd been Leah's best friend and, later, total nemesis. Well, fuck him and his better-than-you attitude.

"Still playing by the rules and doing what Mommy and Daddy tell you, Drew?"

He slammed the Aston Martin's trunk down and glowered at her—all heat and danger and dominance as he stalked toward her, his tall, muscular frame moving with a predatory grace that made her pulse spike and her core clench. She knew that look. Even more, she knew what happened *after* that look. It usually involved ties, orgasms, and promises that would never be kept. For most of her life, her body and her brain had battled it out over Drew Jackson and today was no different. But unlike that summer, her brain won this time and she scurried into the car, shutting the door behind her and locking it for good measure.

The cocky bastard strolled right up to her door and rapped a knuckle on the window. While there was nothing she'd like better at the moment than to drive off, that wasn't going to happen thanks to the tree blocking her in from the front and Drew's truck cutting her escape off from behind. Surrendering to the moment, she rolled down the window.

He rested an arm on the roof of the car and leaned casually against it, his lazy grin not fooling her for a single, solitary second. "I know it'll be hard, Sweets, but try to stay out of trouble while you're in Catfish Creek."

Sweets.

He thought he had the upper hand.

Not today, buddy.

"Whatever you say, Sheriff." With her hands on the wheel, she squeezed her upper arms closer to her body—a move that brought her boobs closer together as it lifted them. It wasn't subtle. It wasn't meant to be. In her experience, subtle went right over most men's heads and she wanted—needed—Drew to remember that he'd been much more than a passive partner that summer. Hey, girls had egos to maintain too. "I'd hate for you to have to handcuff me...again."

Drew's eyes went dark with lust and his nostrils flared before her sanity returned and she rolled up her window, then turned the key in the ignition. He got the hint, stalking off to his truck. Her sideview mirror provided the perfect shot of his smackable ass as he did so and she wasn't woman enough to look away. Half a minute later he yanked the police light off the roof of his truck and pulled out onto the street. She made a three-point turn and headed in the opposite direction toward the service station, wondering how in the world she'd ever thought such an insufferable prick like Drew Jackson could be her one and only.

2

Leah

V asquez's Auto Care was right on Main Street, a short drive off the highway and two blocks down from grease heaven, also known as The Hamburger Shack. Leah had caused a total work stoppage when she'd parked the Aston Martin inside their service bay. With the way Jorge Vasquez and the rest of the mechanics were looking at the car, she kinda felt like a pimp.

Seriously, it was getting a little awkward. The guys were *whispering* to it for the love of Pete.

"I just need a new tire," she called out to the group of men enthralled with the Aston Martin.

Jorge Vasquez looked up at her, made a tsk-tsk sound and shook his head. "Can't do that."

And she thought only her best friend Grayson Cleary was this weird about cars. "Why not?"

"It would be a sin to put a non-manufacturer-endorsed

tire on this beauty." He crossed himself and kissed his thumb.

This was Catfish Creek. Population: Lotsa Crazy. There was no way she'd hear the answer she wanted but she had to ask anyway. "Do you have one of those?"

"Nope."

"Jorge, you're killing me," she said with a groan. "I'm only in town for a few days for the reunion, I don't have time for you to baby a rental car."

"Shhhhhh," Jorge said, looking at the Aston Martin. "Don't listen to her, *mi tesoro,* she doesn't understand you."

Despite her rising frustration, no doubt helped on by her run in with Drew, she couldn't help but laugh at the scandalized expression on the mechanic's face.

Jorge smoothed his hand across the Aston Martin's gleaming hood. "I've already reached out to the rental place listed on the registration to get pre-approval to work on the car and find out who their parts supplier in Fort Worth is. I'll have the tire tomorrow morning, plus, that will give me time to make sure you didn't damage the wheel driving around on a flat like that."

Okay, not the best news in the world, but not the worst either. "Good thing I can walk to the hotel."

He tipped his head back toward where her bag was sitting on a stool near the garage door. "We took your bag out of the trunk and popped everything from the interior into here." He handed her a manilla envelope, his gaze still locked on the Aston Martin.

"You know I'm coming back for the car," she said.

"Yeah, but this way you don't get to the hotel and realize you forgot something." He grinned and gave her a quick wink. "It's small town service. Bet you don't get that up in Denver."

"It's definitely not Catfish Creek."

Not by a long shot. She'd gotten out of town as fast as she could after high school graduation and hadn't regretted her decision once. The fact that her shop in Denver, Botanical Solutions, was only a block away from the garage where Grayson worked made it even better—she got to keep the one part of Catfish Creek she'd liked. If only she was attracted to Gray. Oh yeah, he was cute and inked up and funny, but not even at her horniest had she ever wanted him. Drew on the other hand? Her panties got wet just thinking about him and she hated his guts after what he'd done. That whole Jackson family was nothing but bad news. Principal Christianson had been right about one thing when it came to her, she made some pretty shitty choices--especially when it came to that summer and acting out on the Drew Jackson fantasies she'd had from the first time she'd slipped her fingers beneath her panties and got herself off.

And before she could start thinking too much about the firmness of Drew's ass and how it felt when the muscles moved as he pumped into her, she grabbed her wheeled bag and headed south toward The Hamburger Shack. She smelled it before she hit the front door and by the time she walked through it, her stomach was rumbling for the kind of artery-clogging goodness that came with cheese, bacon and a hunk of red onion sandwiched between two toasted buns and served with a side of spicy fries.

Fifteen minutes later she was two bites into a heart attack when something—or someone, really—blocked the sun streaming in from the restaurant's huge glass window. Glancing up, she took in the no-neck, muscle-bound pseudo cowboys in store-starched Western shirts, jeans, and boots so gaudy only a tourist would even think to pick them up.

Both wore sunglasses. One was blonde, the other had carrot red hair and a dimple in his chin. If they were local or here for the reunion, she'd forsake the homemade lemonade that had come with her burger—and that stuff was liquid gold.

"Table's taken," she said before turning her attention back to her meal.

Blondie snorted. "We see that."

"So move along." She took another bite, chewing slow while watching the men out of the corner of her eye. These two set off a whole passel of warning bells, but she wasn't about to flinch. Botanical Solutions may sell legal marijuana but that didn't mean that all of her clientele stayed on the right side of the law. She'd learned to listen to her danger early warning system.

"Be glad to," Red said as he swiped one of her fries off her plate. "Just as soon as you give it back to us."

She edged her hand closer to the steak knife by her plate. It wouldn't do a lot of damage but jabbing it into one of the Rhinestone Cowboy's softer spots might be enough of a distraction for her to slip past them because she had no fucking clue what they were after. "It?"

"Don't play dumb," Red said. "We know Jessup gave it to you."

Fucking A. This was like being in one of those dreams where she had no clue what was going on beyond the fact that it was probably really bad. "Jessup?"

Red took off his sunglasses, planted his palms on the table on either side of her plate, and leaned forward, not stopping until he loomed over her. "Give it up or pay the consequences."

His breath smelled like stale cigarettes and onion rings. Not a great combination. Keeping her gaze locked on him, Leah curled her fingers around the knife handle and gripped it tight, ready to do what needed to be done to get out of here before 'roided-up Red decided it was time to get really serious.

Movement to her left flashed in her periphery.

"The only one who's gonna be paying is you," Drew said, his hand resting on the butt of his still-holstered gun.

Drew

Paid muscle. It wasn't something Drew spotted every day in Catfish Creek, but he'd run up against enough thugs for hire when he was in Fort Worth to recognize the breed. They were big, cocky, and no doubt had at least one gun concealed on their persons. His money was on their ugly-ass boots since their pearl-button shirts were too tight to hide anything.

"The door's that way." He jerked his chin in the direction of the front door, thankful that the smattering of customers at The Hamburger Shack for a late lunch were more interested in watching the show rather than getting involved in it.

The goon straightened up until he could almost look Drew in the eyes and puffed out his chest. "This has nothing to do with you."

Wrong answer.

"I say it does." *Especially when it comes to Leah Camacho.*

"Don't get your panties in a twist," the guy said as if it were an insult. "We'll be gone soon." He glanced back down at Leah, offering her a cold smile, before putting on his shades. "One way or another."

The men ambled out as if they hadn't just delivered a promise there was no way he'd let them keep. Standing his ground, Drew watched their progress as they exited The Hamburger Shack and got into the extended cab pickup truck that was a match for the one that had slow rolled by Leah's car earlier. He snapped the loop back over his service weapon and noted the license plate number for later—and there would be a later, he had no doubt about it. There always was with their type. He wasn't worried about catching up with them when he needed to later though because it was hard to hide that much douchebaggery in a town this size.

The waitress dropped off a glass of sweet tea just as Drew slid into the chair opposite Leah.

"Thanks, Marsha," he said.

He took a long sip of tea while Leah continued to eat her fries, as if what had just gone down was a normal part of her daily life. Shit. For all he knew, it was. She *did* sell pot for a living.

"You following me?" she asked, licking the dusting of fry seasoning off the tips of her fingers.

Distracted by the sight of her pink tongue and the memories it conjured of what it looked like when she'd used the same technique on the swollen head of his cock, it took a few moments for her words to sink in.

He shrugged. "Noticed the truck from earlier parked outside and figured trouble was stirring. How about you finish your burger and tell me what's really going on."

She gave him a haughty look and pushed her plate away. Stubborn woman. Only place she liked to be told what to do was in bed--and even then sometimes it got a little dicey.

"They think I have something of theirs."

"Drugs?" he asked.

It seemed the obvious choice considering what she did for a living, but judging by the fire in her brown eyes as they narrowed and the snarl that curled up on one side of her full lips he'd chosen poorly.

"No," she retorted with enough attitude to all but give him the single finger salute. "Believe it or not I'm not packing our most popular HEA brand of marijuana to my high school reunion in Texas because that would be illegal."

Testy. It looked good on her. Always had. Every time she'd gotten all riled up that summer, they'd spent fucking each others brains out on any flat—okay, any—surface, the wildest times had always happened when she'd gone all spitfire on him. His cock thickened against his thigh and he had to shift in his seat. Her not-so-subtle glance down and smirk confirmed she hadn't missed his maneuvering.

Fucking A.

"So what do they want?" he asked.

She shrugged. "No fucking clue."

Okay, she didn't trust him to help. That was as obvious as his half-staff hard-on, but he had one week left on the job and he wasn't about to let his jurisdiction go to shit because of some out-of-town trouble hot on Leah's ass. She knew something, she just may not know it. Time to figure it out.

He crowbarred his brain out of the gutter and put it into cop mode. "Where were you before you got to Catfish Creek?"

"Fort Worth to see my mom," Leah answered. "She and my stepdad bought a house there after Shana graduated."

There were five Camacho girls—besides Leah there was Ariella, a bush pilot out in Alaska or somewhere like that; the twins, Meira and Dalia, who had a ranch in Montana; and the baby, Shoshana, who, according to the Catfish Creek gossip mill, was getting a degree at UT—and one brother, Isaac, who'd been a year behind Drew in school. Isaac was a former military special ops type who was in Fort

Worth now working with B-Squad Investigations and Security. Drew had run into Isaac several times while he'd still been working in Fort Worth. All of the Camachos had done like Leah and had gotten out of Catfish Creek as soon as they'd graduated—exactly like Drew had done until that call that came from his mom had dragged him back to town.

"Anything weird there?"

"Beyond the normal Camacho craziness?" Leah laughed. "Not much."

Okay, that knocked out his first and second theories. There had to be something though that would bring in heavyweights on Leah's ass. "After that?"

"I went to the car rental place," she paused, her eyes rounding with excitement. "Now *that* was weird."

His cop instinct started buzzing. "Explain."

She did, giving him a quick rundown of the sweaty guy at the rental car place who'd given her a free upgrade to the Aston Martin. Then, in the middle of describing the shady experience, she stopped dead and smacked her palm against the table.

"No fucking way," she exclaimed. "That thing can't be real."

Failing to come up with the same answer she had, he asked, "What thing?"

She sprang out of her chair and grabbed her purse, fishing out a wad of cash and tossing it on the table. "I've gotta go."

Oh, hell no. He clamped his hand down on the handle of her suitcase. She wasn't going anywhere without him. "You mean, *we've* gotta go."

She rolled her eyes at him. "Fine. Come on."

They hustled out of The Hamburger Shack and he followed her to Vazquez's Auto Care while she ignored every question he hurled at her. Once there, they hurried up to the sidelined Aston Martin parked in the garage, opened the passenger door, and searched inside the empty glove compartment.

"Hey, Jorge," she hollered to the owner, who was watching from the corner. "Did you guys grab the stuff out of the glove compartment when you cleared out the interior?"

"Yep." Jorge nodded. "It's in the big envelope I gave you."

Without another word, she pulled a manilla envelope out of her purse and opened it up. Then, she took out a goofy pink bag with a unicorn on it and emptied its contents into her palm. It was the biggest fake diamond he'd ever seen. At least, he figured it had to be fake.

He took a closer look. "That can't be real."

"That's what I thought too," she whispered. "Until the assholes in the truck showed up at The Hamburger Shack, but who leaves a million-dollar diamond in a glove box?"

Someone cleared their throat. Hand going to his gun, Drew whipped around to face the threat. Two men in matching dark suits stood with their hands clasped in front of them. Everything from their close-cropped hair to the way they held themselves screamed Feds. As if they had it choreographed, they flipped open their wallet badges.

"It's one point six million, actually," the guy on the right said. "I'm Agent Curtis. This is Agent Ritter. FBI. Is there somewhere we can talk?"

Great. Drew swallowed a groan. His life had just gotten a lot more complicated. Why did that always seem to happen when he was around Leah? Still on guard, he stalked over to the men and inspected their badges. They were legit. The Feds had come to Catfish Creek. Lucky him. His last week on the job was supposed to be boring, filled with dumb shit like dealing with Beauford Lynch's eternal war against

Maisy Aucoin's cat. Then Leah Camacho had come squealing into town with what was probably a stolen diamond and what was definitely bad news in the form of two paid thugs on her ass. He let out a sigh and surrendered to the inevitable.

He nodded at Curtis and handed him back his badge. "We can use my office."

"This doesn't involve you," Leah said, stubborn right down to the freckles on her toes.

Ignoring Ritter's arched eyebrow and the smile Curtis was failing to smother, Drew turned his attention to the woman who always seemed to disrupt everything about his orderly world. In her tight jeans, T-shirt and Doc Martens, with her long hair streaming down her back like an invitation to wrap around his fist and hold tight, she was nothing but trouble. And he wasn't about to let her out of his sight anytime soon.

"Sweets," he said, his voice dropping to a lower register that he usually didn't use outside the bedroom. "Don't even try to fool yourself on that one."

3

Leah

If he didn't stop calling her Sweets she was going to...she didn't know what but it would probably involve the hard toe of her Doc Martens. She'd given him the cold shoulder on the ride over to the sheriff's office, only to have him ignore it completely. The man was an ass. And now she had the Feds on *her* ass. Just wait until her brother Isaac found out—and he would. With his connections as part of the B-Squad Investigations and Security in Fort Worth, there was no way he wouldn't.

Keeping that little tidbit to herself, she followed Drew into his office, taking the time to admire the way his ass made well-worn blue jeans look even better as he shrugged on a button up over his white T-shirt. Yeah, it seemed kind of crazy to be mentally drooling over his butt under the circumstances, but 'roided up assholes in big trucks who were obviously compensating for something didn't shake her up. It just pissed her off. And when it came to her and Drew, anger and sex went together like toasted PB and J.

Drew's office could have been a picture in Texas Sheriff's Monthly. There wasn't a single item out of place and absolutely nothing personal about the place, with the exception of one family photo featuring his parents and bitch queen of a sister, Jessica.

"Have a seat," Drew said, gesturing to the three chairs facing his desk as he sat down behind it. "Why don't you guys bring me up to speed."

Nope. That wasn't going to fly. The Rhinestone Cowboys had come to *her*. She wasn't sitting by the sidelines now while the menfolk discussed serious things. This was her life and she wasn't about to be shut out of it—especially not by someone who'd taken her sense of trust and shredded it completely.

"Us," she said, dragging one of the chairs around so it was next to Drew's and facing the agents.

Drew arched an eyebrow. "Us?"

"Yeah, bring us up to speed," she said, sitting down and giving him her best don't-fuck-with-me-fella look. "I'm not just here because I'm cute."

"No, you're not," Agent Curtis said right before the tips of his ears turned cherry red. "What I mean to say is that we've been tracking you since you left the car rental place in Fort Worth."

She froze in her seat. "Why?"

"The fifteen-carat diamond," Agent Ritter said.

Her stomach sank. Part of her—that idiot part that believed things would always work out in the end, even when she knew they wouldn't—had held out hope that the whole thing was just a bizarre misunderstanding.

"It's really real?" she asked, already knowing the answer.

Ritter nodded. "It's the last piece from a massive jewelry heist in Antwerp. We'd been following Ricky Jessup—that's the guy who'd been behind the rental desk. He'd been in on the heist but double-crossed the rest of his crew and walked away with the best diamond in the lot. His fellow thieves weren't particularly happy with him, as you can imagine, and decided to get it back. When he spotted the guys in the truck tailing him, he ditched them long enough to swap your compact rental with the Aston Martin rental he'd been driving. According to what he said before he lawyered up, he figured he'd track you down later using the rental company's LoJack system."

The agent's words swirled around in her head. "So it wasn't the boobs."

Ritter blinked twice. "I don't know what that means."

"Never mind." She wasn't about to explain that she'd figured the rental agent had gone boob-blind when he'd upgraded her. With the explanation for what really happened—and why—taking hold, some of the confused fog lifted, leaving two very important unanswered questions. "Why are you telling me this? You have the diamond now. Why didn't you just arrest the Rhinestone Cowboys?"

"Technically, the diamond is in the sheriff's custody and we need you," Curtis answered.

Drew stiffened beside her, his brown eyes narrowing as he stared down the two agents. "Why?"

"The guys in the truck are low-level," Curtis said. "We want the man who organized the job. And if they think the diamond is in federal custody and they have no chance of getting it back, we have a much harder job at tracking them back to the head of the snake. But if they think you still have it..."

Realization sank in. "You want me to be bait?"

"Only for a day or two," Ritter said.

"No way," Drew said.

The harsh finality in his voice needled her in all the soft spots she'd fought for so long to keep protected. It was a call back to her days when walking down the halls of Catfish Creek High School was like navigating a minefield with people like his sister, Jessica—her former best friend— lobbing verbal grenades for the freak in black, her teachers warning she'd never make anything of herself if she didn't stop hanging out with the losers in the school parking lot, and those losers wondering why in the hell the bitchy brainiac was out there smoking a joint with them. Everyone had loved to tell Leah what exactly she should be doing with her life. It had taken awhile, but she'd finally figured it out on her own and she wasn't about to give up that power to anyone—especially not the man who'd broken her heart as if it hadn't been worthy of special care.

She pivoted in her seat, facing Drew full on, and smiled. It wasn't a nice smile. "It's not up to you."

The vein in his temple pulsed. "You're putting yourself in danger."

"I'm already in danger from the sounds of it." What with the Rhinestone Cowboys following her from Fort Worth and threatening her at The Hamburger Shack.

Drew's hand clamped down on her arm, sending a wave of invisible sparks up her arm that went straight to her clit. "Not if you refuse."

Her nipples puckered against the sheer material of her bra and a lazy wave of desire slid through her. Damn this man. Damn him for having this effect on her when she *knew* better than to fall for it. Desperate to reassert her control, she yanked her arm free, missing the heat of his touch as soon as it was gone.

"Now where's the fun in that?" She turned to the agents. "I'll do it."

Ritter nodded. "We can keep a watch on you, Ms. Camacho, but we have to keep our distance or risk blowing the case. If their past history is indicative of future behavior, then Hank Wynn and Markus Miller, the men following you, won't be aggressive. They tend to use their size for show."

"Don't worry," Drew said. "I'll be right next to her the whole time."

Telling him to fuck off would feel so good that she *almost* gave in to it, but she wasn't that dumb. The Rhinestone Cowboys weren't the regular badass wannabes that she dealt with on an all too frequent basis in Denver. They had FBI agents following them. There was a one point six million dollar diamond on the line. Nicer people than those two would do a whole lot of bad things for that kind of money. If it were anyone else acting as her temporary bodyguard she would have said yes immediately. That it was Drew rankled, but the choice between dealing with him shadowing her when she left her hotel room or facing the Rhinestone Cowboys again on her own wasn't much of a decision.

"Fine," she said, still not liking it even if it was the right choice.

Curtis looked relieved. "Okay, we need to work out some details, take your statement, and outline the plan of action to get these guys to lead us back to the guy in charge. The easiest to deal with though is if you can look off duty while you're with her, Sheriff, so Wynn and Miller knock up the confrontation in the restaurant as just an overprotective male. It's a good thing you're not wearing a uniform today. We need you to pretend to be a friend or boyfriend rather than a guard dog."

"Oh, that won't be difficult," Leah said with a harsh chuckle. "He's played *that* part already."

And he should have gotten an award for it.

Drew

A few hours later, Drew was white knuckling his sanity as he got in behind the wheel of his truck. The drive from the sheriff's office to his house would only take about ten minutes at most, but with Leah steaming in the passenger's seat and shooting him dirty looks, it felt a lot longer. Keeping his hands loose at ten and two on the steering wheel instead of relaxing back and letting his fingers wander over to her long legs like he wanted, Drew watched the road for any signs of the truck Wynn and Miller had been spotted in. The problem was with the influx of new vehicles into town because of the reunion this weekend, Catfish Creek's streets didn't look the same as they normally did.

"What do you mean you canceled my hotel reservation?" Leah asked after he pulled out of the sheriff's office parking lot. "Where am I supposed to stay?"

Ignoring the last question, he kept his tone even as he answered, "Exactly what it sounds like." And he'd do it again.

High-handed? Yep. Smart? Most definitely because when he said he was going to be with her 24/7, he meant it. The woman always seemed to turn his world upside down —especially the last time she'd rolled into town. She'd been nothing but temptation and trouble wrapped up in an off-limits package that he hadn't been able to resist then and was having a helluva time doing so now. Especially when she looked at him like she was now, as if she didn't know whether to fuck him or fight him.

"This is Catfish Creek," she said as he turned left at Sam Houston Avenue. "This weekend is probably the only time every hotel room in the entire town is booked with a waiting list a mile long."

"County fair time," he said, turning right onto Alamo Road and fighting to keep the grin off his face.

A half beat of silence. Then, she leveled one hellacious glare at him. "What?"

He gave in to the smile twitching his lips. God, he loved giving her shit just to watch her spark. "No hotel rooms to be found during the county fair."

She let out a huff and turned away from him to stare out the window. "I hate you right now."

Good that would make what came next easier—even if hearing it was like getting jabbed in the eye with a broken stick.

"Okay," he said, keeping it as neutral as he could.

He turned onto Denton Court and headed straight for the small one-story house at the end of the first block. Halfway there, he pressed the garage door opener attached to his visor.

"That's all you have to say?" she asked, looking around at the neighborhood, no doubt trying to figure out where they were going. "Am I supposed to sleep on a park bench so as to make a better target for the Rhinestone Cowboys?"

"Nope." He pulled into the garage, pulled up until the tennis ball hanging from the ceiling told him his truck had cleared the door, cut the engine, and watched the garage door roll shut behind them. "You're staying with me."

Her eyes went wide. "No. Fucking. Way."

"It's the easiest way for me to keep an eye on you 24/7."

And if there was more to it than that, he wasn't about to admit to it out loud--or in his head for that matter.

Not wasting time waiting for her response, he was out of the truck and halfway through the house with her bag before she caught up to him in the hallway outside the only bedroom.

"You can't be serious," she said, following him into the bedroom.

He tossed her bag in the middle of his bed. "Call your brother and see what he thinks."

Hands on her hips, fire sparking in her eyes, she stared him down. "Why, because I'm a girl and couldn't possibly understand things?"

Girl? She *definitely* was not a girl. Leah Camacho was all woman and he had a raindrop's chance in hell of ever forgetting that. He hadn't forgotten it in the years since their summer together no matter how fucking hard he'd tried. But this wasn't about the fact that he'd never been able to shake her ghost. Her safety was at stake and no matter what had happened between them before, he'd do whatever it took to keep her alive and in one piece--even if that meant breaking himself apart in the process.

"No, because I'm a professional," he snarled, bearing down on her to send his message home. "This is what I do. I keep people safe. Right now I'm going to keep *you* safe. If we had to sell a shitload of pot, then I'd trust you to know the right way to go about it. Until then—which will be never—you need to trust me and do what I tell you."

When she didn't say anything, he reached around behind her, slid his hand inside the back pocket of her jeans, and pulled out her phone.

"What are you doing?" she asked, her cheeks flushed and her voice a little more breathy than it had been before.

Ignoring the way his body immediately responded to her, he took a step back and scrolled through her contacts list. "Calling your brother." He hit the call button. "Maybe he can talk some sense into you."

She swiped the phone away as it was ringing. "I don't need to—"

The muted sound of Isaac Camacho saying, "Hey, sis," sounded from the phone.

She flipped off Drew and put the phone to her ear. "Isaac, I think I might need bail money."

"What do you mean you *might* need bail money?" Isaac's voice came in loud and clear over the phone for that one.

Leah looked directly at Drew. "Because I just *might* kill Drew Jackson."

He laughed. He couldn't help it. She was pissed and it looked fucking good on her. Giving her some space, he walked out into the hall and to the living room and gave it a once over. He didn't need to pick up anything. He'd always been neat. He liked things cleaned up and orderly, which is why his attraction to Leah had come out of left field. Orderly was not her way. She was risk and disarray and taking the plunge without knowing what was coming next.

That summer, after gaining real world experience as a cop in Fort Worth, he was ready to bite the bullet and follow his dad's dream for him and go to law school and become a corporate attorney. It wasn't what he'd wanted but it had been expected. A few whirlwind weeks with her and he'd taken the risk. He told his dad that he was going to law school to study criminal law. His dad had responded by pulling the plug on paying for school. The result was Drew going back to Fort Worth as a cop—this time, permanently. After years of night school, he had his law degree but by then he wasn't just working as a cop anymore, he'd *become* one. Spending his life behind a desk just wasn't in the cards. Even Catfish Creek was better than that. And in a few days, that would be gone too. All he was waiting for was the call from the Fort Worth PD with a start date.

A noise behind him pulled him out of his thoughts and he turned around. Leah stood in the dim hall, the light from his bedroom silhouetting her and outlining every curve.

She held out the phone. "Isaac wants to talk to you."

He just bet Isaac did. He took the phone from Leah. "Hey, man."

"I'll be there in three hours," Isaac said.

"No need. I've got her and the Feds are doing surveillance."

"It doesn't seem right."

Drew shoved his hand through his hair and tried to imagine the fallout if Isaac showed up in Catfish Creek. It wouldn't be good. "You show up here with your B-Squad fire power and you'll put an even bigger target on Leah because Wynn and Miller will know she's got more backup than one guy and it'll make them desperate. People do stupid shit when they're desperate. Right now they still think it's an easy job and will lead the Feds right back to the man running the show. If Wynn and Miller scatter, the head of the snake will just send in more muscle—maybe more dangerous and definitely unknown. Right now, we know who they are and where they are. This is the best plan. She's protected. She's safe."

Drew left out the part about Leah being more pissed off than Beauford Lynch watching Maisy Aucoin's cat prance through his backyard.

"If anything happens—"

"It won't," he cut off Isaac. "You knew me back when we

played ball together in high school and when I was still on the force in Fort Worth. I'm good for this."

Isaac let out a sigh but he didn't argue. He couldn't. Drew was damn good at his job and they both knew it.

"I heard you're joining back up in Fort Worth," Isaac said.

"That's the plan."

"Well, seeing how you're going to guard my sister with your life then I'll buy you a beer when you get back—Lord knows you're gonna need it."

Drew grinned. "I'll be there."

"Just don't fuck this up."

He glanced up at Leah, standing with her back to the hall closet and her arms crossed underneath her luscious tits. His cock automatically started thinking very happy thoughts despite the death glare she was shooting him. Fuck, she might kill him, but Wynn and Miller wouldn't get within touching distance of her. No matter what. "Never."

He ended the call and handed the phone back to Leah, his fingers brushing against hers. That small connection was enough to remind his dick and the rest of him just how good it felt to touch her. She slid her phone back into the back pocket of her jeans and then rubbed her hands together as if she'd felt that sexual charge too. Judging by the way her nipples pressed outward against her thin T-shirt, she had. At least he could take comfort in the fact that they both were waging a war that had nothing to do with diamonds, paid muscle or anything else outside of his front door.

"You always think you know what's best for me," she said. "Isn't that how you put it that summer?"

No one slid the knife home quite like Leah. "And I was right."

They were total opposites. He couldn't understand her. They'd have only made each other miserable if they'd tried to make it work—especially long distance. So when the call came about the job with the Fort Worth PD, he'd gone and left only a texted goodbye.

"Of course." She strode up to him, stopping only when they were toe to toe, her tits practically touching his chest and her luscious mouth within kissing distance. "The perfect Drew Jackson is *never* wrong."

Not when it came to Leah. He'd been right. He knew because if he hadn't, he would have forgotten her long ago. So why was he about to fuck things up? Unable to stop himself, he dropped his hands to her hips and jerked her against him.

"Exactly," he said right before crashing his mouth down on hers.

4

Leah

If there was any sense of fairness in the world, Drew Jackson would suck as a kisser. Really suck. It would be all jabbing tongue and slobbery lips. But as Leah's mama had told her years before, life isn't fair. And Drew's kisses were the kind that short circuited her brain and electrified her body, making her forget everything else but him and how he made her feel. His hands cupping her face, making her skin tingle with anticipation. His lips, strong and hungry against her own, untying a knot of lust she'd kept on lockdown as well as she could around him. His hard body pressed against hers in all the right places as he backed her up against the hall closet door until there wasn't even a millimeter of space between them. His lips moved from her mouth to the column of her throat, making her toes curl inside her boots.

"It's not fair," she said, her voice low and desperate.

He laughed against her skin, a soft tickle before the sharp nip of his teeth against the sensitive spot where her neck met her shoulder. "Sweets, when has that ever been part of the equation when it comes to us?"

The bastard was right. There was nothing but trouble between them, so she might as well get it out of her system once and for all.

Her hands were on his shirt, yanking it out of his pants almost before her brain had caught up. Wasn't that the story of her life though—especially when it came to Drew. She slipped her hand up underneath and her fingers rose and fell over the defined lines of his six-pack abs. It was good, but it wasn't enough. She wanted—needed—to see, to lick, to touch more. Before she got a chance though, he wrapped his hands around her wrists and pulled them up high.

"You're killing me," she said with a groan. God, he loved to play his games.

He adjusted his hold so he held both of her wrists in one hand and reached around behind his back, sin in his eyes and a dangerous smirk on his face. "No, what I'm going to do is much worse."

It was too much for her lust-fogged brain to unravel, right up until he pulled a pair of sheriff's office-issued hand-cuffs out from a loop on his jeans, snapped them around her wrists with a solid click and draped the short, two-link chain between them over the hook extending from the top of the closet door.

She yanked on her arms. They stayed put in their upright, fully extended position. A different kind of heat sizzled across her skin. "You have got to be fucking kidding me."

Smart man that he was, Drew took a few steps back and out of range of her legs. "Are you uncomfortable?"

She narrowed her eyes and glared at him. "I'm pissed."

One side of his mouth curled up as he unbuckled his

belt, drawing her attention down to that part of his anatomy she either wanted to kiss or kick—her brain couldn't decide, but her body had already made up its mind. Warm, liquid desire had her body aching for him even as she couldn't get within touching distance unless he decided she could. Something about that state had her body buzzing.

"You're pissed?" he asked, not bothering to cover up his amusement. "How unusual for you."

"I wonder why when it comes to you."

He answered that with a shrug before taking the five steps it took to get into the living room, laying his handgun on a side table next to the couch, and then coming back to stand in front of her in the hall. His gaze stayed on her face as he began unbuttoning his shirt, but Leah was nowhere near as disciplined. She couldn't stop her attention from traveling south with his fingers as he slipped each tiny button through the hole, revealing the expanse of his chest. She had to bite her bottom lip to stop herself from moaning. His low, throaty chuckle snapped her attention back north to the smug look on his face.

"You're such a jerk." She yanked on her arms. "Uncuff me."

"Not yet, Sweets, I have plans," he said, leaning in close and dipping his head down so that his lips almost touched hers.

Everything went so still as anticipation swept through her that she swore even her heart stopped beating for a moment before starting back up with a rush that had her entire body tingling. Only a last desperate surge of self-preservation kept her from rising up on her tiptoes and falling into the kiss. God, this man undid her. She could do this—do him—and keep her sanity but only if she was careful. Something dark and hungry flashed in Drew's eyes before he blinked it away, breaking the moment, and his lazy smirk returned. He brushed her lips with a barely there kiss, before squatting down and going to work on the laces of her Doc Martens, leaving a mixture of need and confusion in his wake.

He pulled one boot off and tossed it to the side. "Why do you wear these things?" he asked, untying the other.

"They're comfortable." At least they were right up to the moment when Drew decided to leave all the parts of her she wanted him to touch alone in order to take off her damn boots.

He took off the other boot and dropped it with a loud thunk. "They could knock out a bull."

"You know," she said, her frustration at his deliberate pace sneaking into her voice. "In the right light, with your hair a little messed up, you do look like you have horns."

There went that one-sided smirk of his again as he stayed on his knees in front of her and redirected those talented fingers to the top button of her jeans. "Are you flirting with me, Leah Camacho?"

"Not when I'm cuffed to a door when I'd rather be fucking you out of my system."

"Is that what we're doing?" The button popped free, but he lingered, brushing the rough pad of his thumb across the bare skin above her zipper.

Her breath caught as she fought giving in to the moment. A little enjoyment was one thing. Falling back into bad habits was something completely different.

"Could it ever be anything else?" she asked, ignoring the flutter of hope she knew better than to ever listen to again.

Answering with a non-committal shrug, Drew peeled off her jeans, leaving her now very damp panties in place. "How much do you like that shirt?"

"Don't you dare cut it off. It's my favorite." Soft black cotton that hugged her boobs without squashing them against her chest as if it had delusions of being the most unforgiving king of sports bras, her shirt had been on heavy rotation since the spring.

He toyed with the hem, the back of his knuckles skimming across the curve of her belly. "You'll change your mind."

"Cocky bastard." The insult was sixty miles shy of sounding as tough as she wanted but with Drew taking his sweet time about touching her, making her every sense tune into him *and only him*, that was about as badass as she could get at the moment.

"Nah." He leaned forward until his mouth was only millimeters from the patch of skin right above the hot pink bow on her panties. "Confident."

Anticipation thick enough to choke on swirled around them. He was fully dressed and on his knees in front of her. She was half naked, handcuffed to a closet door, and so turned on she was about to have an orgasm even though Drew had spent more time taking off her Doc Martens than caressing any part of her that actually ached for his touch.

His gaze flicked up toward her and something dangerous flashed in his dark eyes that sparked an answering call within her. And in that single moment that stretched to an eternity, she knew--just as sure as the stars were prettier in Texas than anywhere else in the world—that Drew Jackson was nothing but trouble. Even worse? God help her, he was *her* kind of trouble.

Drew

Long legs, big tits, smart mouth, devious fucking brain. He'd compared a lot of women to Leah Camacho since that summer. None had come close. Now he had the real thing and he almost didn't know what to do with her. Check that. He knew *exactly* what to do with her, the question was what to do first.

"You're killing me with these," he said, hooking a finger into the waistband of her hot pink panties. Watching the pulse point in her neck go into overdrive, he nudged the ridiculously girlie material down low enough that he could see she kept everything trimmed but not bare. All the better. "Such a bad girl on the outside with your tough chick boots and badass black, but look at you underneath." He kissed the spot below her belly button. "So soft." Another brush of his lips going lower. "And unless things have changed, which I highly doubt, you are very, very wet."

He stopped right above the line of tight curls, held his breath, and waited for her answer, his cock hard as a lead pipe.

"Yes," she said in a breathless whisper. "Wet."

The temptation to rip the flimsy lace away and lick her slick pussy until she came on his mouth had him fighting for control. "For what?"

"You."

Almost exactly what he wanted to hear. "More specific, Sweets."

"Your tongue. Your fingers. Your big, fat cock."

"All of it, huh?" The scent of her arousal when she rocked her hips toward him made him ache. "Come on, Sweets, you have to say it."

She let out a harsh groan. "All of it."

In one smooth motion, he slid the hot pink fabric down her smooth legs. She kicked them away and spread her stance without him even having to ask.

"You're eager tonight," he said, kissing his way across from one hip to the other, coming close but never quite getting to that one spot he knew she so desperately wanted. "But I have a lot of time to make up for. A lot of fantasies to play out. This," he stood up and wrapped his fingers around each one of her bound wrists, "was one of my favorites."

"Why?" she asked, the word ending with a moan as he kissed and nipped his way down the long column of her neck.

He left the question unanswered, distracting her by grasping one hard nipple poking against the cotton of her T-shirt and rolling it between his fingers while she shut her eyes and let her head fall back against the door. The look of wanton abandon on her beautiful face was almost more than he could take, but she needed to know who was in control here. He was. And if he wasn't, then everything was fucked because no one had ever made him lose control like she had. That was dangerous for his career and his sanity. Cops and pot dealers—even legal ones—didn't make for long-term lovers, especially not when they lived states away from each other.

What the fuck are you thinking, Jackson? This isn't forever. It's tonight. Maybe the weekend. She's gone as soon as the reunion is done, so cowboy up and grow a pair.

Needing to stop his brain from spinning the kind of fantasies he couldn't allow himself to have, he cupped both of her tits through her shirt, squeezing with just the right amount of pressure that had her arching her back in ecstasy. Oh yeah. This is what his girl liked. A little rough. A little loss of control. A little tease and tickle.

"Too bad about this shirt." He lathed his tongue across one of her protruding—but covered—nipples. "I remember just how much you love to have these beauties played with. You were always so responsive when I'd use my teeth, suck them hard into my mouth, rub the hard stubble of my beard against the soft flesh. I understand though. It's obviously a very important shirt."

Leah groaned and knocked the back of her head against the door. "Just do it."

He managed—just barely—not to beat his own chest in triumph. "Do what?"

Giving him a glare that would kill most men, she said, "You know."

"Say it." Asshole? Him? Hell yes.

"Either uncuff me," she yanked her arms, making the cuffs rattle, "or cut my damn shirt off."

Saying I told you so was a temptation he avoided. Leah's legs were still free and, no doubt at this range, she could do some real damage with her knee. So instead, he took a step back and let himself take a long, slow up-and-down look at the one woman who'd gotten away who was now shackled to his hall closet door. That he'd shoved her out of his life with both hands by being a complete jackass wasn't lost on him, but sometimes doing the right thing sucked. No one knew that more than him. Tonight wasn't about the right thing though, it was about rocking her world so she'd remember him with the same ache with which he remembered her.

"Don't worry, I'll save you," he said. "It's all part of the job."

He fisted her shirt, but instead of going to get his utility knife, he slid the soft material up her arms until it was bunched around her wrists and half hanging from the same hook that held her cuffed wrists upright.

Sentimental sucker.

More like horny bastard who didn't want to leave Leah's side long enough to walk over to the kitchen and grab a utility knife.

The view almost made him swallow his tongue. Her tits were perfect. Scratch that. The same boobs on anyone else would be impressive but not nearly as incredible. That it was Leah who he got to touch, to lick, to kiss, to hear moan in ecstasy—that is what made all the difference. Her shirt out of the way, he was confronted with a second obstacle: Her sheer, hot pink bra. Too desperate for any other option, he lifted her tits out of the cups, shoving the material down and to the side and then lowered his lips to her perfect blush-colored nipples. She writhed and moaned as he sucked the bud into his mouth. Refusing to leave the rest of her alone as he grazed his teeth across her sensitive flesh, he slid his right hand lower, sinking between her slick, swollen folds.

"Oh God, yes," she called out, her voice as tight as the rest of her was soft and pliant to his touch.

Fuck. This was better than he remembered, having her like this; hot, wanting and desperate for him to give her exactly what she needed.

"What do you want, Sweets," he asked as he circled a fingertip lightly around her extended clit.

"I want to come."

"On my fingers or mouth?"

"Your dick," she said equal parts sexy surrender and stubborn demands. "I want to feel you inside me."

He glided a finger into her tight opening and then another. She squeezed him hard enough that the head of his already impossibly hard and aching cock became slick with pre-come. Sinking his dick balls deep inside her sounded like heaven right about now, but he'd be done too soon and he wanted to take his time with her. So instead of answering her, he withdrew his fingers from her sweet heat, dropped to his knees. His mouth was buried between her legs, lapping and sucking and teasing as he slipped his fingers again inside her, curling them to rub up against the bundle of nerves right there. This wasn't about finesse. It was an all out pleasure assault. He wanted to take her as high as he could, as fast as he could, before both of them lost their ever-loving minds. Circling her clit with his tongue. Rubbing his beard against her soft flesh just hard enough to tantalize. Fucking her with his fingers while she rode his face like she wanted to get to that orgasm as much as he wanted to take her there. As her moans became higher, he sucked hard on her clit and her thighs began to shake on either side of his head. Then, he added the press of his thumb to the spot right underneath her clit and she broke, her climax tasting sweeter than anything else in the world as he licked her until she begged him to stop.

Looking up at her, as loose and limp as she could be still cuffed to his closet door, his brain and his body went to war. Smart thing was to walk away while he still could. Too fucking bad he never could do the smart thing around Leah.

He uncuffed her and carried her into his bedroom, lying her down on his bed. Her dark hair flowed across the pillows, her naked body open to his perusal. Her full pouty lips were curled just enough to let him know she was up for more—exactly like he'd imagined her in a million jerk-off fantasies. Staying three steps back from the bed, he started to undress.

She sat up, watching him as he stripped off his shirt and kicked off his shoes. "Why do you always want to tie me up?"

"Because nobody runs like you do." It was true. For as much as he always seemed to be standing still and doing the expected, Leah was constantly moving and surprising everyone in Catfish Creek. "You run even when you're standing still. Always on guard. Always primed for a getaway. You've been like that since you were six and spent almost every afternoon at my house playing with Jessica."

Something bittersweet flashed across her face at the mention of his sister's name. "Those days are long gone."

"And thank God for it, because you were an even more stubborn brat then."

She grinned up at him, all sass and sexiness. "Spoken like a man who's not getting laid tonight."

"Sweets." He popped open the button of his jeans and kept his gaze on her hungry face as he slowly lowered the zipper. "We both know that's a lie."

He wouldn't say his ego was small to begin with, but it definitely got a might bigger as she watched him strip. Of course, he played it up a bit, taking his time getting his jeans off and then toying with his boxer briefs before dropping them. She was sitting on her heels at the edge of the bed by the end, sucking that full bottom lip of hers into her mouth, her eyes dark with lust.

"No more cuffs unless I'm locking you up," she said.

He barked out a laugh at that idea. "That's not gonna happen."

One side of her mouth went up, mocking him. "Chicken?"

No. Worse. "I've jerked off too many times remembering the feel of your skin and knowing I'd never get the chance to touch you again to ever give up the opportunity to have my hands on you."

"Show me."

Oh, hell yes, he was going to show her exactly all the ways he wanted to touch her. He took a step toward the bed.

She held up a hand, stopping him. "No. Show me how you jerked off to me. I want to watch."

"Does that get you hot, the idea of watching me stroke this big cock?" he asked, wrapping his fingers around himself and bringing them up and down slowly.

She bit her bottom lip and nodded, her gaze locked on his hand around his dick. Fucking A. There was no way he could say no to her when she looked at him like that.

Leah

She was going to come again just from watching Drew touch himself. Hot didn't begin to cover it. Molten. Face of the sun. Texas in August record-setting heat wave. It was *that* fucking hot. She was tempted to get down on her knees in front of him, but there was no way she'd be able to stop herself from joining in on the fun and she wanted to torture him a little like he'd done to her in the hall.

"Where are you when you stroke your cock thinking about me?" she asked.

"Bed. Shower. Kitchen." Slow and steady his hand stroked up and down his shaft. "On my fucking couch when some actress on TV reminds me of you. Once at work."

Her core clenched at the idea, the taboo of it making her wet enough that she could feel it on her thighs. "What got you that time?"

"It was right after Karly started organizing the reunion. Everyone was talking about it. I couldn't get you out of my head. I kept thinking about that night we fucked behind the stadium. It was so hot that no one was out but us. You were naked and on your knees in front of me, my cock filling up your mouth." He stroked his cock hard right up to the head, milking out some pre-come and scooping it up on one finger, holding it out for her.

She didn't hesitate, she opened her mouth and licked the salty liquid off, managing somehow not to jump him right then and there. "I remember that. I won that bet."

"Nah." He went back to rubbing his dick. "You lost, that's why you were naked and on your knees."

Men were so slow sometimes. "That's what you think."

"Fuck," he groaned and cupped his balls with his free hand. "That makes it even hotter. Just that image of you looking up at me, your lips were bright red and that sound you made every time my dick hit the back of your throat. Damn. It had me so hard I could barely fucking walk to the officer's locker room to take care of things."

Dying to touch him, but refusing to let herself, she fisted the sheets in her hands. "And you did?"

"Fuck yes. I was so close that I stood up in one of the changing stalls with one hand pressed against the cinderblock wall and the other wrapped around my prick." He threw back his head, tension cording his neck. "Three strokes and I was spraying that wall and swallowing every sound I wanted to make at that moment."

"What sound did you want to make?" Her body ached for him—all of him, filling her up until there was only them. Somehow, this had turned from tormenting him a little to outright torture for her.

"A groan. A yell. Your name."

She couldn't look away from his hand speeding up and down his swollen cock. "You're close now, aren't you?"

"Fuck yes." The words were as rough, hard, and desperate as the look in his eyes.

God, this man. Even like this, there was something so commanding about him that made her want him in ways she hadn't ever wanted anyone else. Without thinking, she leaned forward and cupped her boobs. "I want it right here."

His hand sped up. "You wanna be marked."

By him? Yes. "I want to be sticky with you and then I'm gonna rub it into my skin while you watch."

"Fuck, Leah," he yelled as he came, spraying her breasts with his hot release.

True to her word--and loving that bit of something extra that he always brought out in her—she rubbed it into her skin as he watched, his eyes almost black with desire and his chest heaving for breath.

Drew

If he didn't walk away now, Drew was going to die a miserable, horrible death alone because she was going to ruin him for anyone else. This woman wasn't just trouble. She was a certifiable menace.

And she's in your bed.

Naked.

Slick.

Beautiful.

Ready for more.

"Damn, Sweets." If it came out like a man who'd had a

prayer answered, well, he couldn't be held accountable for that right now. Not with her.

One eyebrow went up. "You say that like a man who'd rather be somewhere else."

"Not on your life."

Cupping her face in his hands, he leaned down and kissed her, exploring and tasting every bit of her—or at least as much as he could tonight. He came down on the bed beside her, drawing her in against him. Her soft curves always fit so perfectly against him. Hands and mouths were everywhere as they each laid claim to the other one last time. He couldn't get enough of her. Neither could his dick because he was already hard again.

"What are you, secretly seventeen?" she asked, circling his cock with her fingers and squeezing him tight.

"Around you? It seems like it."

Reaching across her, he pulled open the drawer of his nightstand, took out a condom and then rolled it on. Looking down at her as she lay on her back spread out before him, his breath caught. Damn. If this was what trouble looked like, felt like, then maybe he did need a little more of it in his life.

"It's always like this with you, Sweets."

"Ditto," she said with a shy smile before pushing him down to his back and straddling him. "Now fuck me."

When she lowered herself onto his rigid cock, he could have died a happy man. Her warmth tightened around him and desire tightened his balls. Pleasure rippled outward from where they joined. He clapped his hands down on her round hips and yanked her down harder as she rocked her hips forward and back. Small whimpers escaped her lips as she increased the pace, riding him hard and fast in smooth, deep strokes. It was good. Really fucking good. But he needed more. Now.

He rolled them both so she was on her back and thrust deep into her hot, tight pussy. His eyes rolled back with pleasure as pressure began building in his spine. Her hips met his every thrust, words made incoherent by lust escaping her lips.

"Leah." Her name came out in a strangled groan. He couldn't hold on much longer.

She undulated against him and squeezed, her whole body tensed as she came around his dick with a cry. His balls tightened and he buried himself to the hilt and came so hard his vision went black and if he never got it back it would be worth it.

Chest heaving, he rolled onto his back and got rid of the condom, dropping it in the trashcan near his bed. Then he reached out, wrapped a hand around Leah's waist and pulled her close. Every bone in his body had been replaced with Jell-O laced with some sort of sleeping pill. He was going down. Hard. But a sharp elbow to the ribs kept him from drifting into the sweet hereafter.

"Hope you don't think you're staying here," Leah said, all the sex kitten gone from her voice.

He tried to untangle that statement and came up blank. "What?"

She rolled over to face him, her still kiss-swollen lips drawn tight. "That didn't change anything. I still hate you."

Drew glanced down at her naked body, lingering on her tits that still bore the tell-tale signs of him. "But you want me."

She let out a huff and shrugged. "Seems to be my cross to bear."

This woman made no sense. None. They'd just had

mind-blowing sex and she was kicking him out of bed? Out of his *own* bed? Whatever he'd been thinking during the deed, he needed to block that shit out because Leah Camacho was exactly the same as she'd always been.

"You're as mean as a snake-bit cat in a room full of rocking chairs." Still, because he'd been raised right, even if it did piss him off sometimes, he got out of bed and gave the space to his houseguest.

She smiled up at him, obviously not giving a shit. "And I own it."

He grabbed a pair of sweats from a drawer and yanked them on. "Sweets, you're gonna have to learn one of these days that there's nothing wrong with being a little soft around the edges."

"Sure there is. That's exactly how you get hurt, which I don't plan on being again—especially not by someone with the last name Jackson."

The soft tremble to her voice, despite the hard look in her eye and her do-not-fuck-with-me body language, hit him like a punch to the gut. Leah and his little sister Jess had been best friends growing up but something had changed all that. He didn't know what, but it had obviously messed with both of them. The realization took some of the edge off his own frustration as he started out the door.

He stopped in the doorway. "People can change, you know. You gotta learn to trust that." Maybe even him.

Whatever reaction he'd been hoping for—and he wasn't even sure himself—he didn't get it. Instead, Leah harrumphed and rolled over so she faced away from him.

Shaking his head, he walked out into the hall, grabbed a blanket from the hall closet where his cuffs still hung, and made up the couch in the living room unable to get the idea of change out of his head. People did change. But him? He was still in the same place he was last time Leah was in town, dealing with overbearing parental expectations of what he should be doing and waiting for a phone call with a job offer out of town. It was like his life was stuck on a loop with Leah being the one who always seemed to knock him out of it.

5

Leah

Thank God the coffee pods were right by the Keurig because, if not, she might have staged a one-woman riot in the middle of Drew's kitchen. She'd brass balled her way into having the bed to herself last night, but that didn't mean he hadn't been there anyway. He'd invaded her dreams to the point that she'd woken up this morning with her arms wrapped around his pillow and her nose buried in it as she inhaled the amber, musky scent of him that clung to it. That meant she was pissed off and horny at the same time—both of which were all too familiar when it came to being near Drew.

After half a cup of straight black goodness was warming her belly, she felt human enough to make the call. The contact list on her phone listed the number as being for Isaac, but her big brother wasn't the person she wanted to talk to. She hit dial.

"B-Squad Investigations and Security," a woman answered, her familiar voice as crisp, efficient, and borderline bitchy as the woman herself. She and Leah were like peas in a pod that way.

"Hey, Tamara." She sat down at the table and took another sip of coffee.

"Leah, is everything okay? Isaac just left on a job but I can patch him in." His brother's fiancée immediately ready to burst into action after Isaac had no doubt brought her up to speed on the craziness going on in Catfish Creek.

"Nope." She shook her head as if Tamara could see. "I was looking for Lexie."

"Really? Why?"

"Tamara, I know you love my brother and even if you didn't, you know he's got a way of crowbarring the truth out of people." And she didn't want the favor she was about to ask Lexie repeated to her big brother.

"Don't I know it," Tamara said with a chuckle.

"So it's better if you don't know the answer to why."

There was a pause long enough for her to look around Drew's sunny kitchen and realize that, like his office, it was completely bare of anything personal, as if he'd never unpacked when he'd moved in.

Tamara sighed. "Secrets are not the basis of a strong relationship."

"Are you telling me you two have always told each other everything?" The silence on the other end of the phone was telling. "It's not like I'm hiding a sixteen year old."

"That was just the once and I had a good reason."

Yeah, like the girl's megalomaniacal cult leader father who was dead set on forcing the girl to marry one of his middle-aged followers. "No argument."

"Fine," Tamara said with a huff, finally giving in. "Hold on."

B-Squad didn't have on hold music. It was just a series of

rhythmic beeps. She'd counted fourteen beeps when Lexie, the resident computer guru and cat aficionado, picked up.

"Leah, what kind of trouble are you causing now?" Lexie asked, as always more than ready to hear the latest bit of gossipy crazy.

"What makes you think I'm causing trouble, Lexie?"

"Because I know you and your brother," Lexie said, the sound of her fingers click-clacking across the keyboard coming in loud and clear over the line. "If trouble isn't everyone in your family's middle name then I don't have a slight cat obsession."

"You're calling an entire wardrobe of cat T-shirts and enough kitty figurines to make a certified cat lady think you had a problem as slight?"

"I'm quirky," Lexie said. "So sue me."

"I'd rather put you to work."

"What've you got?" she asked, going straight into all-business mode.

"Two dirt bags, Hank Wynn and Markus Miller. They're involved in some kind of diamond theft ring. I want to know everything about them and anything about who's in charge of the crew."

"Doesn't sound like idle curiosity to me. You need me to come down and bring some of the B-Squad toys?"

Leah wasn't sure whether to be thankful or annoyed that her brother's B-Squad crew had adopted her as one of their own. For a girl with trust issues, it took a little getting used to.

"Nah, between the Feds and one big-dicked sheriff I have enough babysitters already."

"Big dicked as in has a big dick or acts like one?"

Leah thought about it as she took another sip of coffee. "Both."

Lexie laughed. "I want details the next time I'm in Denver or you're in Fort Worth, whichever happens first."

"Deal. I need any info you can find on Wynn and Miller fast and quiet."

"No big brother heads up, huh?"

"There's a new cat T-shirt in it for you."

Lexie snorted. "You really think there's one I don't have?"

"You have a Captain Ameri-cat one?" Leah asked, picturing the one she'd seen in a random email that had landed in her inbox. "It's a cat in a Captain America suit saying he fights crime one evil hairball at a time."

"I'll have everything including their favorite color of underwear by breakfast."

Leah smiled. "You're the best, Lexie."

"Don't you know it."

She hung up and downed the last third of her coffee. If there was anyone who could make that promise and keep it, it was Lexie. Not for the first time she wondered what the story was behind the cat-obsessed computer genius, but shoved it aside. She had to deal with the here and now before delving into any other mysteries. The sound of a man clearing his throat behind her made her jump out of her seat.

Drew stood in the kitchen doorway wearing a scowl and a very tiny blue towel slung low across his hips. Water droplets clung to his chest and she watched, unable to look away, as one drop made the downward trek across his hard abs to disappear behind the towel. It was enough to make her brain short out.

"What in the hell was that?" Drew asked, stalking toward her.

She swallowed past the sand pit in her mouth and—out of a sense of primal survival desperation—moved so the small, round kitchen table was between them. It wasn't that she was afraid of him. More like she was afraid of what she wanted to do when she was near him—every dirty thing she could possibly imagine.

"I'm moving things ahead."

He glanced down at the table and back up at her with a knowing smirk. "And how were you doing that?"

Her cheeks burned. Damn it. Why was it always like this with him? Taking a deep breath, she clicked together her bad attitude, using it as a shield against his cocky charms. "I called in a favor to get more information about the Rhinestone Cowboys."

He spread his legs wide and crossed his arms over his broad chest. "You don't need to know more."

His stance couldn't have screamed "I strong man, you weak woman" any more if he tried.

This wasn't how she worked. Drew, of all people, should know that. She wasn't about to entrust her life to some random FBI agents who were more concerned with catching the man in charge rather than keeping her safe. And Drew? She might be physically safe with him, but emotionally was a whole other story. The best way to save herself was to get this whole cat and mouse game over with as quickly as possible, so that was exactly what she was going to do.

"I'm not going to sit around Catfish Creek and wait for those two goons to make their move."

"That's the stupid plan the Feds came up with and you agreed to." He shoved his hand through his wet hair, making it stand up as he rounded the table to her side.

Her pulse picked up as he neared and desire warm and slick sent a shiver of anticipation through her body. Her nipples hardened automatically with his closeness, as if they'd been trained to sit up and take notice of Drew. Hell, with the way he played them like a maestro they had. She couldn't control her body's reaction to him and it pissed her off as much as it turned her on. He really was the one man she'd never been able to stop herself from wanting, which is exactly why she had to fight against it so hard. She couldn't trust him, that lesson he'd taught her oh so well. That pinprick of humiliation and hurt was enough to pull her back from the edge of desire and back to the problem at hand.

"I'm not going to sit back and wait for the other shoe to drop. That's not the way I roll."

"No, you just roll over everything in your path without any thought about the consequences, but there will be some if you do anything idiotic like try to draw Wynn and Miller out without backup."

"All the more reason why I can't wait for the Feds to do their job." Frustration over the situation and her body's reaction to the half naked man in front of her, she pushed past him, her only goal being to get out of the kitchen before she did something she'd regret, "I'm going to get ready. Until I know my next move I have to act like everything's normal. That means picking up my high school reunion welcome packet and saying hi to all the bitches who think I slept my way through the entire varsity football roster and the assholes who started that rumor in the first place."

"If that's the way you feel about coming to the reunion then why are you even here?" he asked.

Stopping in the doorway she glanced back at him. He had one hip propped against the table and the top of his towel had slunk down low enough she could see a few dark hairs curling over the edge. The temptation to walk back over and drop to her knees in front of him hit her like a sixty-mile-per-hour gust of wind. She could fuck him. She could suck his dick. She could tease and tempt and toy with him until they both were nothing but mush, but she wouldn't be able to walk away happy after that. That summer after graduate school had taught her that. When it came to her heart, Drew Jackson was danger in a tight pair of Levis. He always had been. He always would be. She could pretend she'd come back to Catfish Creek to flip her classmates the bird but that was a lie, she realized in a rush. She'd come back to see him.

"Why come back?" she asked. "To see if anything had changed."

Without waiting for his response, she turned and marched to the bedroom her chin high and her step faltering only a little bit.

Drew

He'd never thought of the cab of his truck as small before. It sure was with Leah in there making the whole place smell like strawberry shampoo instead of Whataburger or The Hamburger Shack. He stopped at one of the lights on Main Street a block from the high school. She didn't look up from her phone. Here he was acting as her well-armed chauffeur and she'd ignored him and spent the ride so far to the Catfish Creek High School texting. She let out a giggle that was so unlike any sound she had ever made around him before that he missed that the light had turned green until the driver behind him let him know with a prolonged honk.

"Something funny?" he asked, with a little more snarl than he meant to put in the question.

She didn't even look up. "Just Gray."

Grayson Cleary. The guy had been in the same class as Leah and Jess. Up until now he'd seemed like an okay guy. The unfamiliar prick of jealousy stabbed him in the left eyeball. "The dropout?"

Finally, she looked up from her phone, but only to cut him a glare. "You mean my best friend?"

"Since when?" Girls weren't friends with guys. It just didn't work out that way. If the chick was hot—and Leah was beyond that—then the dude wanted to bang her. End of story.

Her jaw went tight. "Since your sister blackballed me in school and Gray was the only one who stood by me."

There was just enough of a tremble in her voice to make him hate what was going to come out of his mouth next, but it had to be said. Jess could be a real bitch, but she was still his sister. "I'm sure there was a misunderstanding."

Leah laughed. It wasn't a happy sound. "Nope, no misunderstanding. Pretty, perky, perfect Jessica Jackson declared war and I'm sure she still thinks she won. As if I cared what she did."

"Sounds to me like you still do." He slammed his mouth shut before he could add that it *had* been ten years and pulled into the high school parking lot.

After pulling into a parking spot near the gym doors and turning off the engine, he pivoted in his seat. Leah's cheeks were beet red. This wasn't the spitfire response he loved to get from her. It was hurt. Probably embarrassment. More than likely a whole lot of half buried resentment. His gut twisted. Shit. He was an asshole.

She let out a slow breath and gave him a cold smile. "Well, if this isn't deep thoughts with Drew Jackson."

Over her shoulder he spotted Catfish Creek's own Ms. Gossip watching. Karly Stocker, reunion organizer and all-around rumor monger, was not someone he wanted anywhere nearby while Leah was fighting to get ahold of whatever lurked under the surface of her bad girl defenses. Too bad fate had other plans. Karly was click clacking her way across the hot asphalt parking lot in heels and full-on big Texas hair.

"We've got company," he said, jerking his chin toward the oncoming assault.

Leah glanced out the window. "Oh God. That's Karly, isn't it?"

"Yep." The one. The only. The permanently annoying.

She whipped back around. "Can we just drive away?"

He understood the feeling, but Karly was closing fast. "Too late."

They got out of the truck and Drew hustled around to the passenger's side, getting there at the same time as Karly.

"Well," Karly said with a smarmy fake smile. "If it isn't Leah Camacho as I live and breathe, and with Drew Jackson no less." She gave Leah an innuendo-heavy wink as if they were old friends. "Don't tell me that it's finally happened."

Crap. What had he missed now? "It?"

Karly laughed, an ear-piercing sound that just might cause an epileptic seizure in dogs. "Everyone knows Leah here has been in love with you since she was knee-high to a jackalope."

Next to him, Leah kept her mouth shut but her chin went a few inches higher and her don't-give-a-fuck mask slammed down into place. Everyone had known? Maybe everyone but him. Before that summer, he'd never noticed her as being anything other than the girl in black who used to hang out with his sister.

"Tell me." Karly leaned in, clutching a manilla envelope

with L. Camacho scrawled across the top of it close to her chest. "Are you two *together*?"

"Nope," Leah said, a big, shit-eating grin on her face. "We're just fucking,"

Drew groaned. Karly's eyes went wide. Leah turned and looked up at him as if she was about to fuck him right there against the side of his truck. Karly let out a little hiss of a squeak. *Oh hell.* That was going to be all over town before dinner.

Turning back to Karly, Leah asked, "Is that my welcome packet?"

Gaze ping-ponging between Drew and Leah, Karly nodded and handed it over.

"Well then," Leah said, accepting the envelope and turning back toward the truck. "Nice seeing you."

"Wait," Karly said, her voice a few octaves higher than normal. She paused, took a deep breath, and pasted on that fake grin of hers before continuing. "We need your help."

Leah stiffened beside him, her body all but screaming "hell no." Why in the world she decided to come to the reunion if she was going to ignore every single person there was beyond him, but he was done with it. It was time to join in. He took her hand in his and gave it a quick squeeze before turning his attention to Karly.

"What can we do for you?"

The other woman's shoulders sank with obvious relief. "I need two people to hang the decorations up high in the gym. I can't climb a ladder in these shoes."

Leah glanced down at the other woman's ridiculously high heels. "So take them off."

"And go barefoot?" Karly gasped. "In public? No, thank you. I'd rather go into hiding than go out without my shoes and best lipstick."

Drew cut in again before Leah could make another astute, if snarly, observation. "We'd be happy to help."

"Thank you, glad to see someone in this town still does the right thing. Follow me." Without waiting for a response, Karly took off toward the gym doors, her heels wobbly on the uneven asphalt parking lot.

"Why am I doing this?" Leah asked under her breath as they followed behind.

Knowing just how she'd react to the real reason, he had to think fast. "Because wherever I am, you are until Wynn and Miller make their move and we take them down—and while I'm sheriff in pretty much name only at this point, I still need to act the part."

She snorted. "Always doing what everyone expects of you but when do you ever do what you want?"

He jerked to a stop, halting her progress since they were still holding hands, and yanked her close so that her curves fit perfectly against his hardness. "Does last night count?"

Her eyes went dark and her lids dropped to half staff. Then, she bit down on her full bottom lip making it look almost the exact same way it had last night when she'd come hard around his cock. Suddenly, helping with the high school reunion decorations started to sound like an even worse idea. Karly's high-pitched "yoo-hoo" didn't help. The sound was enough to obviously knock Leah back to reality though.

She blinked, gave him a smart-ass smirk, and tugged him along with her as she strutted next to him toward the door. "You're so romantic."

"Well, like you said." He dipped his head lower so his lips were nearly touching the shell of her ear. "We're just fucking."

~

Leah

Okay, helping out wasn't horrible. Celeste from Leah's honors calculus class was there and they'd gotten to catch up. A few other people who she didn't remember very well, a few who never would have spoken to her in school, stopped by her and Drew's section of the gym to say hello. It was...nice and kinda fun. Now that was a strange thing to experience in the hallowed halls of Catfish Creek High School. Maybe Drew was right. Maybe she did need to open herself up to the possibility that people changed, God knew she had.

Of course, that little realization jerked her attention right back to the man currently starring in every one of her old high school sex fantasies that had rushed to the forefront thanks to her ever horny subconscious. The bastard knew exactly what was going on in her head too. He'd found every excuse to trail his fingers across her skin, hold her hips in the guise of steadying her on the ladder, and "accidentally" grazing his palm across her ass. Finally, she had to take a step back using the lame excuse of wanting to get a big picture view of the decorations they'd been working on from across the gym.

Lame? Yes.

Necessary? Oh yeah.

Her phone vibrated. Leah didn't have to look to know who was making her back pocket buzz. She'd told Gray she'd meet him at The Grange. She was the one who'd pushed him into coming to the reunion. Why? Because she may wear big girl panties, but that didn't mean she wanted to face all of her high school demons without her best friend at her side.

Of course, all of that was before she'd discovered a fifteen-carat diamond in her rental car glove box and had mind-meltingly good sex with the only man she loved and hated in equal parts. Okay, maybe hated was too strong a word. Made her nuts? Drew Jackson definitely did that—and he wasn't about to stop as long as she was figuratively cuffed to him. Just the reminder of handcuffs made her wrists sore and other parts of her tingle to life as she stared at his perfect ass going up the ladder to hang decorations. She was already searching for a somewhat secluded spot to drag him off to before her brain caught up with the bad ideas trying to hijack it.

Girl, you have got to get your head clear.

Her ass buzzed again. Gray. He was just the person to help her screw her head on right. Without giving herself time to think of what could go wrong—sexual frustration mixed with desperation was like that—she pulled out her phone and opened her Uber app. There was a car two minutes away. Perfect.

She swaggered over to where Drew stood next to a ladder looking down at a box of decorations. "I'll be back in a few."

His eyes narrowed in the way only a suspicious cop could carry off. "Where are you going?"

"To talk to Gray." She held up her phone, intimating that she was gonna make a call. By the time Drew figured it out, her ass would be on a bar stool at The Grange.

Drew's hand cupped the curve of her waist, the pad of his thumb brushing the bare skin above her jeans, sending jolts of electricity straight to her clit. Her breath caught. Her pulse sped up. Anticipation sizzled in the air between them, as hot and dangerous as a live wire. She licked her lips and pressed a hand to his chest as she rose up on her tip toes—a loud wolf whistle cut through the gym followed by friendly laughter. Leah whipped her head around. Most of the people in the gym were watching. Her feet fell flat to the floor as embarrassment beat her cheeks.

"I gotta go." The words sputtered out.

Drew grinned and let his thumb dip below her waistband for half a second. "Don't go far."

She just smiled and backed away. Quick. With any luck her Uber would be waiting outside the high school's front doors.

A quick ride with a chatty driver later and she was walking into The Grange. There was a pool hall in the back, dance floor to the right, and the world's jerkiest mechanical bull. The place even smelled the same—like stale beer and good times. Damn. She'd missed this dive. A quick scan of the dim interior and she spotted Gray's dark hair and killer smile. He was such a little hottie and her life would be a million times easier if she was even the slightest bit attracted to him, but he was her bestie, her brother, her solid constant. Anyway, there was a nice girl out there for him and he'd find her eventually. If he didn't, what hope was there for someone like Leah?

As she was walking toward him, she spotted two things. One: Kate, a girl they'd gone to high school with, in super cute leather leggings sneaking peeks at Gray. Two: The Rhinestone Cowboys a few tables beyond Gray near the pool tables. *Shit. Nice thinking ghosting out on Drew, you idiot.* This was not good, but at least they hadn't noticed her yet. Of course, they would in a hurry if she didn't stop Gray before he hollered out her name like he looked to be about to do.

"Hey, sorry I'm late." She rushed to his side, knowing her smile had to look a little on the crazy side but unable to get her face to calm the fuck down.

"It's fine, want me to order you something?" Gray cocked his head and gave her a considering look. "You doing okay?"

Fine? Well, she wasn't currently on fire. That was good. Why had she ditched Drew? Were the FBI guys outside? It wasn't like she could walk out the door and holler "Yo, FBI dudes." *Slick move, girl. Way to go.*

"I'm fine." She waved him off, her gaze darting over to the Rhinestone Cowboys' table. Both were too caught up watching the perfect heart-shaped ass of the waitress who'd dropped off their beers to pay attention to anyone who walked in the door—for the moment. She needed to get out of here. Fast. "Actually, I can't stay. I need to...I just need to do a rain check. Okay?"

Gray gave her a hard look. "You going to tell me what's going on?"

Oh yeah. Like her life wasn't shitastic enough without dragging her best friend into her mess.

She leaned over him, grabbed his mug, and chugged the rest of his water before putting the empty glass down on the bar top. "Can't right now. But I will."

"You know I'm always here for you, right?"

Now wasn't that enough to melt her cold, black heart. "I do, Gray, I do. Now, why don't you stop talking to me and look around at the pretty woman with those fantastic leather leggings who keeps staring at you."

"What are leather leggings?" he asked, a divot of confusion in-between his eyes.

Dudes. So fucking clueless. "They are nirvana. Stretchy and sexy." She winked, unable to stop herself from teasing him. "My new motto."

Gray let out a groan. "Dear Lord, never say that again."

"Seriously though, Kate is looking hot tonight. And I hear she's single." Her phone vibrated. One glance down confirmed a fourth text from Drew. Yep. Sheriff was pissed. She had to get out of here and back to the high school before his head popped off or the Rhinestone Cowboys spotted her. "Anyway, gotta run. Have fun!"

Without giving Gray a chance to stop her, she hustled out the door and into the bright late afternoon sunlight that temporarily blinded her, which explained why she didn't see trouble coming until it was too late. An arm wrapped around her waist and yanked her backward against a wall of rock hard muscle.

"Sweets," Drew's voice held a dark edge as he held her in his iron grip. "Didn't your mama ever teach you it's not polite to ditch your date?"

A shiver of anticipation glided across her skin as a quick blast of desire expanded out from her core. She snuggled her ass against Drew's thickening cock before her brain caught up to what her body was doing. She froze and gave her brain a second to catch up.

"I told you I was going to talk with Gray," she said, the explanation sounding dumb even to her ears.

"Uh-huh." He loosened his grip a fraction but didn't let go. "Try selling that story somewhere else."

"The Rhinestone Cowboys are inside."

He stilled behind her. "Which means you're not about to go back in," he said, something dangerous in his voice she'd never heard before now that made all her girl parts perk up with a hopeful sigh. Then, as quick as he'd grabbed her, he let her go and moved up so they stood next to each other. "Good thing you have other plans tonight."

"I do?" The images that flashed in her mind almost made

her blush and she couldn't wait to try every single one of them out.

"Yeah." He slid his palm across the small of her back and guided her to his truck. "It's family dinner night at Casa Jackson."

Her gut churned. That was definitely not the answer she'd been expecting. In fact, it made the prospect of going head to head with the Rhinestone Cowboys sound totally doable. "Oh, no."

"Oh, yes." He opened up the passenger door. "Even if I have to drag you kicking and screaming and handcuffed to me you're not getting out of my sight again."

Ditching Drew wasn't an option though. He'd cuff her, she didn't doubt it for a minute—and part of her was hoping he would.

∿

Drew

Somewhere in hell the devil was laughing his tailed little ass off. His mom and Leah sat opposite each other at the Jackson family dining room table. He sat opposite an empty seat. Oh yeah, there was a place setting for his father but he'd stopped deluding himself about his old man's dedication to family eons ago. Saying the stilted conversation and long silences were awkward was like saying he only *kinda* wanted to drag Leah into the closest room with a door and relieve some of the stress stringing him tight since she'd dipped out of decorating duty at the gym.

"So Leah." His mom, Jennifer, set her fork down, leaving exactly half a baked potato, half a steak and half her vegetables untouched—just like they'd stay for the rest of the meal. "You sell drugs?"

Drew almost choked on his medium rare steak.

"I operate a fully-legal marijuana shop in Denver, yes." Leah responded without an ounce of emotion in her tone, almost as if all the shit he'd been giving her for her choice in careers had beaten some of the fight out of her.

He hated that. As soon as he got her alone, he'd apologize.

"What an...interesting life you must lead," Mom said, smoothing her hair, a nervous gesture that had become more frequent since she'd gotten out of rehab.

Leah nodded and took a bite, chewing with more effort than her mashed potatoes required.

Yeah, this was going even worse than he'd expected, but dinner with his mom wasn't a responsibility he could ignore. Keeping his head down, he shoveled in another bite of potato

Dinner at his parents' house had never been fun, not even when he was a kid. There was always some passive aggressive fighting going on between his functioning alcoholic mother and his philandering father. Not that they'd ever divorce. Too public a scandal. Instead, they just seethed silently and spent as much time apart as humanly possible —right up until his mom decided to spend twenty-eight days at the "spa" and came home with a twelve-step program that didn't include telling a single soul in Catfish Creek where she'd really been. The price tag for that? Drew had to come home and help her with her cover story. Faced with the choice between seeing his mom get better, even if she was still the queen of the perfect facade, or watching her lose herself in a bottle, he'd done what he'd always done. He'd given up the policing he loved, came home to Catfish

Creek and done the right thing. And with Jess across the country and his dad all but missing in action, there was no one else to do it but him.

"You know, Jessica will be here on Thursday," Mom said. "She's coming from Hollywood."

"How nice for her," Leah said, sounding about as happy as a woman facing a firing squad.

Either oblivious or just too deeply attached to the reality she'd created in her head, his mom nodded in agreement. "Yes, all those big stars really depend on her. Now, if she'd just listened to me when I advised her about what she needed to be doing in L.A., well, she'd be one of those big stars but that girl never did listen. I think it was because of who she hung out with, and look, now here you are with my son."

Like an unexpected slap across the face, the words hung in the air. Grinding his teeth together, he smacked his palms down on the table on either side of his plate and stood.

Leah spoke up before he got a chance, her voice carefully neutral. "I'm leaving town right after the reunion."

"Mom." The single word sounded more like a threat, but both women at the table ignored him.

"Your poor mother," Mom went on. "All of her children have abandoned her. I'm so glad that didn't happen to me."

"Mom. Stop." He smacked his open hand on the table. She loved to do this whole concerned but still evil thing with him and Jess, he wasn't about to let her do it with Leah. "Stop it right now."

"No, it's the truth," she said, her body practically vibrating with the same twisted righteousness she'd had back in her drinking days when she'd lecture him and Jess about the importance of always presenting the perfect family picture. "You're always here doing what needs to be done for family."

Yeah, and didn't he just love every soul-sucking moment of it. And when the call came for the job in Fort Worth, would she just give in and drop back into the bottle? Guilt ate away at him with all the delicacy of a long horn steer tearing through a glass shop.

"And what about what's best for him?" Leah asked, her voice soft but with a strident undertone.

That made both him and his mom stop. Best for him? That was usually the last thing on the long list of keeping the family together that he'd had since his mom brought Jess home as a baby and then proceeded to celebrate the birth of her second child by getting quietly drunk on vodka mixed in with her sweet tea while his dad continued his affair with his secretary. Taking care of the family had always been Drew's first priority, one that had spilled over into the rest of his life where he'd chosen to go into public safety. His brain didn't work any other way.

"Well," his mother said, reaching for her wine goblet of water with a shaky hand. "What's best for family is best for everyone in that family, don't you think?"

Ten minutes later and finally out of the house he'd grown up in, Drew couldn't shake the question as he drummed his fingers against his truck's steering wheel and waited for the stoplight to turn. For her part, Leah was quiet, staring out the window at the people eating at one of the outdoor restaurants on Main Street. He'd opened his mouth at least half a dozen times since they left his parents' house but no words came out—probably because he had no idea what they should be. However, the silence screaming in the truck wasn't it though.

"I'm sorry about my mom," he said, pulling away from the intersection and turning left toward his house.

"Why?" Leah asked. "That's how your mom has always been, drunk or sober."

His jaw dropped. "You knew?"

She snorted and shook her head. "You think you're the only one who Jess called for a Dr. Pepper moment?"

Dr. Pepper had been his and Jess's code for help for as long as he could remember—usually called out because of their mom's obsession with perfection or their dad's casual indifference.

"I thought you and Jess stopped being friends in high school."

"We did but there was history between us." Leah let out a harsh breath. "Isn't that always the case when it comes to the Jackson family and doesn't it always come to bite me in the ass?"

Yeah. He wasn't going to touch that last part right now. "What happened with you and Jess?"

She shrugged. "Just high school girl things."

If that was the case, he didn't see how it would still bother her this much ten years later. "Just spit it out."

Leah chewed on her bottom lip and continued looking out the window at the passing businesses, her shoulders hunched and her arms stationed protectively in front of her stomach. Figuring she was just going to ignore the question, he lapsed back into silence as he turned toward a more residential section of town.

"We'd drifted apart our first year in high school," Leah said, keeping her gaze turned away from him. "Jess fit in perfectly with the popular cheerleader set. I did not. It was awkward, but not horrible, even if I didn't know what I'd done wrong to lose her as a friend. Then, one night our freshman year after she had a big fight with your mom, she called me. We met up at the park by my old house and talked for hours about everything. It was like we'd never stopped being friends. I thought everything would go back to how it was." She paused and drew in an unsteady breath. "I couldn't have been more wrong. The next day at school I made the mistake of saying hi to Jess when she was with some of her new friends. She didn't just snub me, she gave me this look like I wasn't even good enough to be the dirt on her shoe. Then, she asked her friends if they heard the ghost of a total loser talking. They walked off laughing while I stood there like she'd punched me right in the gut. After that, it was war. We were both guilty of firing shots. Sugar in a car tail pipe. Nasty gossip scrawled on the bathroom walls. Clothes going missing from gym lockers. Rumors. Innuendo. General assholery."

"What happened after that?" He didn't know shit about being a teenage girl, but that sounds like just the sort of thing that would have wrecked Jess if it had happened to her.

Leah's chin went up another few degrees. "We graduated and I left this town for good, or so I thought."

Yeah, right up until the summer after she'd gotten her master's degree and there he was all ready to bang her and leave as soon as he'd gotten that call from the Fort Worth PD. If it hadn't been for her encouraging him to see beyond his family's demands back then, he may have just toed the family line and followed his dad into the corporate world where he screwed people over for a living. And how had he repaid her? By leaving her in his rearview mirror without even a goodbye kiss. He'd been young but that was no excuse for being that big of a dick.

"I'm sorry."

She twisted in her seat, one eyebrow up. "For what?"

"For being one in a long line of Jacksons to fuck you over." He turned onto his street, determined to make sure it wouldn't happen again. "Look, don't ditch me again. You could really get hurt."

"I won't." Her arms tightened around her middle even as she got that look in her eye that only meant trouble. "But I'm not sitting by idly, either."

"So we'll do it together." Mind made up, he was already rolling through the scenarios and building a plan as he hit the button to open the garage.

"You mean it?" The surprise in her voice punched him right in the balls.

"Yeah, I do." He pulled into the garage and cut the engine. "It's the right thing to do."

And it was. Not just to make it up to Leah, but because she was right. Sitting around like a breathing target wasn't going to keep her safe. As long as the ringleader thought she had the diamond instead of it being in the sheriff's office evidence lock up, she was in danger and he couldn't have that. It was time to go on the offensive, which meant keeping his hands to himself and his mind on the mission instead of Leah's perfect ass. So, once inside, instead of giving into the call of the sway of her hips or the undeniable *thing* zipping between them, he offered her a curt goodnight. Then, he left her standing in the bedroom doorway, a confused look on her face, as he made up the couch for another night of lower back agony that was still less painful than the guilt and regret about his behavior that was eating him from the inside out.

6

Leah

The next morning, Leah was on the cranky side after Drew's unexpected hands-off goodnight and was yet again staring down the coffee machine when her cell buzzed. However, unlike yesterday, she wasn't alone and Drew was dressed—too bad.

He paused mid-bite in his inhaling of a mountain of bacon surrounded by a valley of scrambled eggs. "Is that your contact?"

"Yeah." She tapped the answer button and set the phone down in the middle of the kitchen table, then sat down next to Drew, trying to ignore her body's instant awareness of him as he scooted his chair closer to hers. "Hey, Lexie, what did you find out?"

"Ugh," Lexie groaned. "Am I on speaker? I fucking hate being on speaker."

"Sorry," Drew said. "That's because of me."

"Oh, I like that voice," Lexie said. "Is this Mr. Big Dick?"

Leah almost spewed her first sip of coffee everywhere.

"Yeah," Drew said, glancing up at Leah and giving her a sexy smirk. "That's me."

Cheeks burning at Lexie's usual lack of filter, Leah got the conversation back to where it was supposed to be. "So, what can you tell us about Wynn and Miller?"

Drew's raised eyebrow let her know that he was probably going to bring the whole big dick thing up again. Of course. Because this is how her life worked in Catfish Creek, home to all of her top ten most embarrassing moments.

"Both are more muscle than brain," Lexie said at a fast clip, no doubt used to giving these types of bad guy briefings to the other B-Squad agents. "If I was going after a fifteen-carat diamond, I sure as shit wouldn't be leaving them unsupervised—especially not if the person I was selling to was half as pissed as it seems Mr. Moneybags is."

Drew's head jerked up.

"Rewind, Lexie," Leah said.

"Okay, Wynn and Miller work for Warren Law, nice irony, right? Officially, he's in the import/export business but instead of cocaine along with his shipment of antiques, he dabbles in hot jewels. He's as dirty as a Jeep after you've taken it mudding but he's non-violent—not even a whisper of him using the muscle twins for anything other than general intimidation, which is probably why they haven't jumped you already. Law has a reputation for patience. Too bad he's under the gun this time. Warren had a buyer all lined up for the diamond, a buyer who doesn't take no for an answer and likes to outfit people in cement shoes. So poor Warren has to get that diamond or go to Mr. Bent Nose and explain why he doesn't, which—in all likelihood—will end very, very badly for him."

"How do you know this?" Skeptical didn't even begin to

describe the cynical look on Drew's face. "The FBI isn't even sure who Miller and Wynn work for."

Lexie's snort came through loud and clear over the line. "I've got skills the Feds wish they had."

"And a tendency to hack her way into places she's not supposed to be," Leah added.

"Yeah, well, if those guys would share information a little better their lives would go so much more smoothly," Lexie retorted.

Drew shook his head. "That's never going to happen."

The import/export was a great cover for a jewel thief. In a weird way, Leah couldn't help but kind of admire the guy for putting such a solid front in place that even the FBI hadn't figured it out. All they had to do was figure out a way to get to him and get him on the record admitting to the diamond theft. After that, the FBI would step in, arrest him, and she'd be free and clear.

"So your thinking is that Law is here in Catfish Creek?" Leah asked.

"I'd bet my miniature hand-blown glass feline collection on it."

That was as good as a guarantee. "Have any goodies to share?"

"Always," Lexie said. "Pics and a down and dirty brief is already in your inbox."

"Thanks, Lexie."

"Catch you next time you're in Fort Worth," she said. "I want all the details about Mr. Big Dick with a good voice."

Drew's eyebrow arched. "I have a name, you know."

"And a hot official photo too, Sheriff Drew Jackson," Lexie said with a laugh.

"Never get a job in the real world, Lexie." Leah shook her head, wondering not for the first time how Lexie—a legitimate Texas heiress and all around quirk fest—had ever ended up at B-Squad Investigations and Security. "You'd be fired in a heartbeat."

"Probably. Toodles, kids."

After Lexie hung up, she and Drew sat and drank their coffee in silence for a few minutes. Leah assumed he was working his way around to the same solution to Law as she had. She was wrong.

"You spend a lot of time in Fort Worth?" he asked, pushing the last remains of his breakfast around his plate with his fork.

"My mom's there with my stepfather. My brother's there with his fiancée. I go back every two or three months."

"Ever think of moving back down?"

A short bark of a laugh escaped. "Not unless Texas gets a political makeover and pot becomes legal. Believe it or not, I like what I do. I like the people. I like the challenge of running a business. I like that I made a move into a kind of business that a lot of people who got their business master's at the same time as I did wouldn't touch with a twenty-foot pole—not that they aren't regretting it now."

"So why not apply those skills to another kind of business?" he asked, snagging her cup of coffee and stealing a drink.

Letting the question soak in for a minute, she tried to find some of the nose-in-the-air judgment he'd used before when asking about her business, but it wasn't there. It was like he was just...curious. The realization did something to her insides, filling her with a soft warmness she wasn't used to and didn't know how to process. So she did what she always did in that situation and made herself harder.

"Because I like selling pot." She jerked her chin higher and straightened her spine, not letting herself drop eye contact. "It's not just the hipsters who want to get high. It's a legal product that a lot of people enjoy. It's also a Godsend for folks with glaucoma, cancer and other illnesses. Plus, it's fun as hell to show up to work in my Doc Martens and T-shirt and scare the shit out of the uptight suits who stop in on a regular basis and try to buy me out."

"You always did love standing up to the man," he said before finishing off her coffee.

She snagged her now empty cup from him, her fingers tingling at the contact and her nerves more than a bit jangly at this new side to Drew, and walked over to the coffee maker to start another cup. "Talk like that makes you sound like a Baby Boomer burn out."

"I'm an old soul."

"Nah, just one who thinks there's only one path and is going to shoehorn himself onto it no matter what," she said as she turned and watched his jaw tense. Shit. The snark had just popped out. Drew was wrong, she didn't just run when cornered, she built defenses out of brick-sized attitude mortared together with bitchiness. That needed to change. If being here in Catfish Creek had taught her anything so far it was that she really needed to let all the old shit go— including the hurt that had festered since that summer with Drew. "Sorry, it's not my place to say anything."

"If you didn't, no one else would," he said, his shoulders tense. Then, he got up and cleared his spot, loading the dishes into the dishwasher in silence. After clicking it closed, he leaned one hip against the counter and watched her as she drank her coffee. "So we can't let Law get the diamond."

"Agreed," she said, relieved to be back on familiar ground.

"But that doesn't mean he shouldn't think he is."

She couldn't help her grin because she just *knew* this was gonna be good. "Go on."

"We set up an exchange, but we'll only give it to Law."

Oh yeah, she liked it. "Because it's the only way to guarantee Wynn and Miller won't hightail it to the buyer themselves and leave us vulnerable to Law's retribution."

"Exactly." He nodded.

"I like it." She looked up at him, a new appreciation for him softening her defenses. "You've got kind of a devious mind."

"Nothing of the sort. I just believe the shortest distance between two points is a straight line."

"That and a pair of handcuffs," she teased.

His gaze dropped to her mouth. "They never hurt."

Anticipation made her heart beat faster as he took a step closer, almost within touching distance. His focus never left her mouth. Sparks turned the air around them electric. She forgot to breathe, forgot to blink, forgot everything but Drew. Every nerve in her body buzzed with expectation. He was going to kiss her. She wanted it. God, did she want it. Her mouth parted as her body ignored the SOS her brain was sending out. She'd regret whatever was coming next after this was over, when her life was back to normal and she was back home in Denver. This sort of craziness was just part of life in Catfish Creek. His head dipped lower. She tilted her face up.

And then, nothing.

Muttering something that sounded a lot like "fuck me" under his breath, he stepped back and rubbed the back of his neck with his hand.

Her breath came back into her lungs in a whoosh, along with confusion, frustration, and annoyance. He wanted her. It was obvious. The other night had proved that beyond a reasonable doubt. Yet, last night he sent her to bed alone without a second glance and now he denied their attraction again.

"Why are you doing this?" she asked, unable to keep the rawness from her voice. "Why are you helping me?"

He turned away from her and looked out the window above his sink, his profile as hard as the countertop he was white knuckling. "Because I catch bad guys, that's what I do."

It's not what she'd been asking and they both knew it. "And that's it?"

She hated how fucking hopeful she sounded, like she'd come back to Catfish Creek and was once again that insecure girl from high school who hid behind her bad girl persona.

His jaw muscles flexed, but he didn't turn toward her. "There can't be anything else."

And she was still enough of the girl she'd been to wish like hell there could be. So before she could say anything that would even remotely hint at that, she turned and marched out of the kitchen, her chin high, knowing the bad girl sway of her hips would be reflected in the window so Drew couldn't miss what he was walking away from—again.

Drew

Dealing with the FBI was close to the top of Drew's do-not-want list, but there wasn't a way around it. Agents Curtis and Ritter were in his office wearing matching dark suits and blank expressions. That didn't bode well for what was about to happen next considering he and Leah had just finished tag teaming the explanation of their plan.

After a solid ten seconds of silence, Leah looked at him and shrugged before turning back to the agents. "And that's the plan, so speak now or forever hold your peace."

"No," Ritter said.

Yep. That was about the reaction Drew had been expecting. For the Feds, there was no good idea unless it was their idea.

"Excuse me?" Leah asked, fire sparking in her eyes.

That was his girl, always fixin' for a fight.

Curtis seemed unimpressed. "We don't know where you got this information from."

"A confidential source," Drew answered, the less details the Feds knew, the better.

"Someone here in Catfish Creek knows the inner workings of one of the world's most wanted jewel theft rings?" Curtis didn't bother to keep his skepticism below the surface.

Drew put a hand on Leah's thigh before she could say whatever scathing thought was formulating in her head and gave her a soft squeeze to warn her not to push too far. "We never said he or she was local."

"I don't like it," Ritter said.

Leah rolled her eyes. "You don't have to, you just have to stay out of the way."

So much for sending her subtle signals.

"That's not how the federal government operates," Curtis deadpanned.

"And don't I know it," Leah said with a sigh.

Both agents narrowed their eyes. Knowing just how effectively Leah could burrow under a man's skin and make him nuts, Drew squeezed her leg again—harder this time.

"You're not helping," he said half under his breath.

Leah shot him a glare. "I'm not trying."

Of course not. That's not how Leah worked, she was all bad girl attitude, devious brain and sass. He loved that about her. Nothing about her was easy. A man had to work to make it past her defense—and he was determined to do that.

"Here's the deal," he said, turning to face the agents, giving them the look he usually reserved for subordinates who were slow to understand the way things were going to work from now on. "We—really, she—found out more in twenty-four hours than the however long it's been that you've been working this case. We're doing this. You're either coming along for the ride and the collar or you're sitting on the sidelines when I bring Law tied up with a bow to your boss."

It wasn't just the career boosting that came along with credit for a collar that cops—no matter their affiliation—wanted to take the bad guys off the street. It was in their cop DNA. That didn't make letting someone else take the credit any easier because egos were alive and well in anyone who had the power to throw someone in jail, but unless he'd pegged the agents wrong, they'd take the deal.

"Fine," Ritter said, his tone gruff. "We go with your plan but if the whole thing blows up in your face we won't be held responsible."

Drew managed to keep his self-satisfied smile under wraps. "Understood."

Two hours and one massive mission-planning session later and Drew and Leah walked into The Grange, the most likely spot to find Wynn and Miller, according to Lexie's briefing report that detailed the men's habits. Really, the woman was something else, weird cat obsession aside, because there were Wynn and Miller, sitting at a table in the back. Judging by the harried, I'm-about-to-stick-a-knife-through-your-eye look on the waitress's face, they'd been there for some time and had not been the most pleasant of customers.

Following the plan they'd come up with, he intertwined his fingers with Leah's and they walked together across the bar, past the dance floor, and to the men in their matching pale blue Western shirts with pearl buttons so new they still had the folding lines from the store.

Leah gave the duo a slow up and down before shaking her head. "Some people shouldn't be allowed to dress themselves."

"You don't have to fight it, darling, I know I look good," Wynn said, his bright red hair slicked back and held in place with a pound of hair gel.

Stepping in before Leah could tell Miller and Wynn what she really thought of their outfits, Drew cleared his throat, drawing everyone's attention to him. "We want a meet with your boss."

Miller slunk back down in his seat, his gaze twitching left before jerking back to Drew.

"What boss?" he asked.

"The one who keeps you in tacky shirts and cheap belt buckles," Leah said.

"Girlie," Wynn sprung from his seat with more grace than a bulky guy his size usually had and loomed over Leah, "you need someone to teach you better manners."

Drew didn't think. He just reacted, grabbing the man by the shirt and shoving him back against the wall. Half a heartbeat later his forearm was pressed up against the guy's throat hard enough to make Wynn's eyes a little watery. Using his peripheral vision to keep watch on Miller, who was glued to his seat with his palms up in surrender, Drew leaned in and got right in Wynn's face.

"Let's not lose focus, asswipe, because you're too dumb to realize that that lady is the only person keeping your head attached to your neck. Your boss. A meeting. Set it up. Now."

He tossed the sputtering Wynn back into his seat.

"Fine, dang, man," the redhead said as he took out his phone and started texting. "There's no need to go all *Training Day* on me."

He and Leah stood, hip to hip, while they all waited for a return text from Law. There was no way he was giving up the high ground advantage to these two dipshits. They might not have a record for violence and so far they didn't seem to have any skill that didn't involve grunting in the gym, but that didn't mean he was going to let down his guard. Not with Leah here. So the four of them just stayed there, giving each other stink eye, until Wynn's phone finally buzzed with a response.

Wynn picked it up and read the message with more speed than Drew would have given him credit for.

"He wants to know why," Wynn said.

"Tell Law that we'll only hand over the diamond to him," Drew said, sticking to the plan and playing the heavy. "We don't trust you two to carry out your end of things."

Miller made a soft squeak of protest. "That's just shitty."

"Tell him," Leah said as she jabbed a finger into the back of Wynn's shoulder blade.

The redhead shot Leah a dirty look but put his oversized thumbs to work. Again, they waited. This time the answer came back almost immediately.

"Noon tomorrow," Wynn said. "The closed up gas station at the corner of First and McMurray. Just you two."

"Great," Drew said, taking a step back from the table, making sure Leah did the same. He didn't want her within arm's reach of these two if they decided to change their M.O.s. "You can go."

"We were sitting here having a beer," Miller muttered.

"You were annoying your waitress," Drew said, jerking his chin toward the waitress who was watching the goings on from the safety of the bar. "Get moving before I find an excuse to knock your heads together."

Wynn and Miller grumbled like old men kicked out of the Bingo parlor for spitting tobacco on the floor. Drew didn't relax until they cleared the door. Curtis and Ritter would take over surveillance of Law's muscle after that, in hopes they went straight to him. If it worked out that way, great. If it didn't, they were ready for what came next. Now there was nothing to do but wait. And stare at Leah. And think all sorts of porn-worthy ideas for them to bide the time until the meet.

His cock twitched and started to thicken against his thigh at the mental image. Fuck. This is exactly what he'd told himself he wasn't going to do. Still, his hand was in the air as he signaled to the waitress for two beers. A minute later two ice-cold bottles of Bud were on the table.

"You off the clock?" Leah asked as she lifted the bottle to her red lips and took a long swallow.

"We're celebrating." Yeah, that almost sounded reasonable.

"You didn't answer. I know you're not in uniform because of the Rhinestone Cowboys, but you haven't been since I rolled into town."

He glanced down at his daily staple of white T-shirt and jeans. "For all intents and purposes I'm off the clock as sheriff permanently."

"You quit?"

"I was acting sheriff after Sheriff Finnigan had a heart attack, but I lost the election to take it on full time."

It had been the best and worst day of his life all rolled into one. The truth was he needed to get out of Catfish Creek. His mom had enough sobriety under her belt to not need him watching over her. Scratch that. What she really needed was to have the confidence to watch out for herself and kick his cheating ass father to the curb.

Leah's already big eyes went buggy. "Who wouldn't vote for you?"

He laughed and took a sip of cold beer. "All the folks pissed that I wouldn't let little Jimmy and perfect Paula get away with underage drinking, routine violations and other bullshit."

"Didn't they realize they were appointing Mr. Law and Order?"

The way she said it made it seem like he should be wearing a cape and a mask. The image made him crack a smile despite the shitty reality of the situation. "I guess they thought those rules only applied to some folks."

"Wow," she said with a chuckle. "You must have made them nuts."

Now that was the understatement of the year. "Yep."

"So what now?"

He glanced around the bar, taking in the handful of customers eating chicken tenders and downing a quick beer after a long day at work. Nothing out of the ordinary—and maybe that was part of the problem for him. The job with the Fort Worth Police Department seemed ideal, but was that just him falling into another familiar cycle? For a man who never thought much about the big picture of his life, he couldn't help but realize over the last few days that he was in one helluva rut. One that he probably wouldn't have realized if not for the tornado of trouble that was the woman sitting across from him.

And he couldn't have her. Not for real. And that was beginning to be a spiky bur under his saddle so he did what any good kid who'd grown up with a functioning alcoholic parent would do. He deflected. "We enjoy the win while we can."

Leah took a sip of her beer. "Doesn't sound like you've had a lot of those."

"Not as many as I thought I'd have when I graduated high school." Shit. When he'd graduated a few years before Leah and his sister, he had thought the world would be his within five years. He'd been wrong, so very wrong. "The truth is, life doesn't always turn out the way we expect it and it sure doesn't give you any do-overs."

She smacked her bottle on the table, sending foam over the lip and nailed him to his seat with a challenging look. "So you force it to."

"Wow." He laughed. "You almost sound like a woman who doesn't have a Texas-sized chip on her shoulder."

"I don't," she said a little too fast for either of them to be fooled.

"Really?" He took a drink of beer, watching her over the rim. "Then why'd you come back to the reunion? The truth."

He didn't expect her to answer, but once again she did the last thing he'd figured. She straightened her shoulders and gave him what sounded an awful lot like the truth.

"To show them I wasn't the woman they all thought. That there was more to me than just trouble."

How many high school expectations were they both still running from all these years later? He was the responsible one who'd never take a chance, the one voted most likely to uphold law and order. Leah? She was the bad girl with a devious, quick brain she'd probably never use for good. It was past time both of them got over that. You could go home again, but there was no reason why they had to be those people they had been just because they were once again where it all had started.

Fuck this. He was breaking out of his rut.

"Come on." He stood up and jerked his chin toward the empty pool room. "Why don't you try to kick my ass in pool?"

"Try?" She stood up, all sexy confidence and determination.

He smirked. "I'm feeling lucky."

She rolled her eyes and turned, leading the way to the pool room. His gaze went to her perfect, swaying ass like a magnet. Damn. It almost hurt to look at her. It definitely was awkward to walk after looking at her. Looked like he was going to have to get off the hamster wheel of his life and do something about that and, maybe, see what other possibilities awaited.

Leah

Leah didn't need to bend at the waist and lean quite so far across the pool table to make the shot. She did anyway. Getting a good look at the solid red ball as it dropped into the corner pocket wasn't why. It was because she could feel Drew's hot gaze on her as sure as a branding iron. They made a good team and it was nice to see that wasn't only the case in the bedroom—although that's where every single one of her thoughts was ending up.

"So you came back home and Jess stayed out in Hollywood?" she asked, following up on their getting-caught-up conversation.

"There was more to it than that, but yeah." For once his gaze was on the pool table and not her ass or her boobs as she leaned over the green felt.

Someone was keeping things to himself. Was Drew Jackson keeping a deep dark secret or was it something as simple and devastating as remorse?

"Do you ever regret it?" she asked, almost completely meaning his decision to come back to Catfish Creek but she'd be lying to herself if she said that was all of it.

He took a slow sip of the single beer he'd been nursing, his focus still on the pool table. "Yeah, but I can't change the past." He refocused his attention on her, sending a delicious shiver down her spine. "What about you? Ever regret moving up to Denver?"

She gave half a second to the idea of living anywhere else but Denver before sending up a quick thank you that she didn't have to worry about ever moving back to Texas. "Nah. I love it up there. It gets crazy cold, sure, but the people are great. I love being near the mountains after the total flatness of Catfish Creek."

He made his shot, sending the cue ball flying across the table into the trio of striped balls. "So what, it's just you and Gray?"

"Believe it or not, I can make friends, but yeah, we hang out." She came around to his side of the table, nudging him out of her way with her hip, relishing the spark of attraction that led straight to her clit.

"Anything serious?" he asked, a rough edge to the question.

Pulling back from taking her shot, she turned to face him. With one hand on her hip and the other wrapped around the pool stick, she gave him a slow up and down while awareness crackled between them. "Why, Drew Jackson, are you asking me if I'm fucking my best friend?"

"Yeah." He nodded, lust turning his eyes dark. "I am."

Straight and to the point. She'd always appreciated that about him—among other things.

"No." She shook her head, her lungs suddenly unable to take a decent breath. Maybe it was because her bra had mysteriously become too small. *Or because you're flirting with fire, Leah girl.* "It's never been like that for us."

Someone must have put money in the jukebox stationed between the dance floor and the pool tables, because an old school country song came on. It wasn't one of the slow ones or one where someone had been done wrong by everyone but their dog. It was a sing-along drinking song, the kind that included a repeated chorus and sly lyrics that had always made her giggle. This time wasn't any different. Without thinking about it, she laid down her cue on the pool table and started dancing as she sang along.

Drew watched for a few beats before wrapping an arm around her waist and swaying to the music with her as they both sang along. Heat pooled between her legs as her breasts brushed against his chest, his fingers drifted lower on her ass, and that magic *something* between them took ahold of both of them. Before she knew it, he'd maneuvered them so that her back was against the wall in the one blind corner of the bar by the storage door. No one could see them here.

"I'm glad," he said, his lust-hooded gaze dropping to her mouth. He took another small step forward and pulled her hard against him, his hand now cupping her ass completely

Her pulse sped up and her panties all but went up in flames. "About what?"

A new song came on the jukebox. This one was about the boy who'd gotten away. She refused to read too much into that and instead gave in to the way Drew made her feel when he wasn't breaking her heart.

"You and Gray. I'd hate to have to pound his face in." With one of his legs planted firmly between hers so she couldn't help but grind against his thigh, he moved to the song's slow but relentless beat.

"Are you jealous?" she asked, going for light, but ending up more breathy than anything else.

She was about to tease him with another snarky remark but the dark, brooding look in his eyes made her breath catch. This wasn't a dance anymore. It wasn't a teasing encounter. This was more. What exactly that was she had no frickin' clue but it couldn't be worse than last time he'd made her feel like this. She wouldn't let it. A man could only break her heart so many times before she learned her lesson.

"A little," he admitted grudgingly.

She cocked a brow and glanced up at him—well, as up as she could considering a ray of sunlight would have a hard time getting between them at the moment.

"Okay," he said, his voice rough. "A lot."

His mouth crashed down on hers, hard and demanding. That little admission had cost him and now he wanted to be paid back for it. That was okay. She liked the way he expected his debts to be paid. God, she was desperate for him to touch her but his hands stayed locked on her ass as he rocked her against his thigh. Opening under the weight of his kiss, she relished the way his tongue swept inside, taking her higher. This. This is what she ached for. Not just the touch. But the man. Drew. It was almost too much to process. Heat and desire and need built up like an electric ball in her core, throbbing and growing with every move. Then, he glided his lips down the sensitive column of her throat.

"Jesus, Drew," she panted, half surprised she could even form words. "You're killing me."

"What's wrong, Sweets." He nipped at the spot where her neck met her shoulder. "Do you need some relief?"

"Yes." The sooner she could get him somewhere private and rip his clothes off, the better. "Let's get out of here."

"Don't worry," he said, one hand slipping between them and going straight to the button of her jeans. "I'll give you what you want, but it has to be here."

That's not good.

He popped the button open.

She stilled—her body so tuned into him that she almost missed the sound of people and beer bottles clinking in the main bar area.

"Someone could come in," she said, logic fighting through the haze of lust making her entire body buzz with anticipation.

"Yep, it's after work." He nodded and tugged down her zipper. "The town is filtering in so you'd better hurry because we're not moving away from this wall until you come."

Not here. She tried to form the words, but nothing came out. He slid his fingers underneath the elastic waist of her lace panties and brushed against the swollen tip of her clit. *Oh. My. God. Forget everything else. Yes.*

"Oh, you are so soft and wet for me," he said, moving his fingers in a tight circle around her sensitive nub, the friction of her jeans against her plump, slick folds only intensifying the sensation. "Does this mean I should dance with you more often or are you always like this for me?"

She arched into his hand, her answer more of a breathy moan than anything else, "Always."

"Fuck. I love that."

His fingers moved faster as the heel of his palm pressed against the spot right above her pelvic bone, intensifying every sensation zinging through her. Her body tightened as she climbed higher and higher toward that moment of bliss.

Her head fell back against the wall, her eyes squeezed shut as the pressure mounted. "I'm so close."

"That's good, Sweets," he whispered in her ear. "The pool league meets here every Wednesday night. They'll be here any minute." His fingers went into overdrive against her clit. "Oh hell, Sweets, you just got more wet. You like the idea of maybe getting caught, don't you? Well, you're gonna get caught if you don't come all over my fingers right now."

His touch combined with the threat of discovery sent her over the edge and she came hard, biting her bottom lip to keep from calling out. Chest heaving, she tried not to melt into a puddle on the floor of The Grange's pool room. She didn't even have the wherewithal to get annoyed at Drew's knowing chuckle as he zipped and buttoned her pants for her. Cracking her eyes open, she watched as he sucked her juices off his fingers.

"Damn, you're sweet," he said with a wink.

Those three words were all it took to get her from zero to one hundred in a heartbeat. "Let's get out of here."

Nodding at the pool league regulars filtering in, they made it out of The Grange and into Drew's truck in record time. They were almost to his house when his phone rang.

"Yeah?" He listened for a minute, the vein in his temple pulsing faster and faster with each passing second. "I'll take care of it." Finally, he ended the call and turned into his driveway. "I have to go take care of something. Curtis has been tailing us from the bar. I'll let him know to stay here with you. Don't open the door to anyone but him or me and don't you dare go anywhere until I get back."

"Why," she asked, reaching across the bench seat to run her hands up the inside of his thigh and over the hard outline of his cock. "Would you spank me?"

He clamped his hand over hers and curled her fingers around as much of his dick as the position allowed. "Sweets, I'm gonna do that anyway."

Forget her panties. Her jeans were soaked now too. "I thought you were off duty."

"The mayor's war against his neighbor's cat is a different story," he said, shaking his hand.

"That is so Catfish Creek."

"No kidding."

With a final squeeze of his cock and a hot kiss that curled her toes, Drew walked her inside the house, did a quick walk through to make sure no one was there, insisted she lock the door behind him, and then headed out to fight the cat scoundrels of Catfish Creek. Watching him drive away gave her a sense of deja vu of that summer, but this time was different. This time he wasn't leaving for Fort Worth without even a goodbye. This time he was coming back, which meant more to her than she wanted to admit to herself.

7

Drew

The scene at the mayor's house wasn't chaos, but it was pretty damn close. The local librarian, Maisy Aucoin, was in the middle of Beauford Lynch's front yard armed with a cast iron frying pan and a cat that looked like it had gone through at least eight of its nine lives in the past hour. The distinct stench of burnt fur carried on the early evening air. Beauford and his wife, Betty Sue, stood on their wraparound porch each armed with matching shotguns with Mr. Right and Mrs. Always Right etched onto the barrels in decorative script.

It was almost eight o'clock before Drew and two deputies got everyone back on their own property and unarmed. Another half hour and he had Maisy Aucoin's statement and was sitting in the most uncomfortable chair ever in the Lynch's front room trying not to lose his temper at the mayor, who was one windstorm away from having his brain's screen door knocked loose.

Drew pinched the bridge of his nose, let out a slow

breath, and tried again. "Beauford, you lobbed a firecracker at Miss Maisy's cat—and it was a cherry bomb. Beyond being illegal, it was very dangerous." Not to mention idiotic, but mentioning that part wasn't going to make anyone's life any better.

Beauford's fingers played a nervous drum solo on the arm of the couch he was sitting on. "It just slipped out of my hand."

Of all the bullshit answers, that one was as lame as it was a bald-face lie. A lit illegal firework just happened to slip out of the old man's hand and fly thirty feet across his backyard in the general direction of the fleeing tabby cat. The only thing that had saved the fur ball was the fact that at seventy-six, Beauford's aim sucked and he'd missed his mortal enemy by at least three feet.

"This is Texas," the mayor blustered. "A man's allowed to protect himself and his property."

From a ten pound cat?

Shaking his head, Drew took out the citation booklet he'd grabbed from his truck's glove box and flipped it open. "Cherry bombs are illegal under federal law."

"Well, whoop-de-friggin-do," the mayor said, his tone more than a might snarly.

Drew glanced up. The stubborn old goat was sitting with his chin cocked and his arms crossed with the certainty of privilege wrapped around him like a blanket. Any other day and Drew would have just written the ticket, done his duty, and made sure everything looked good just like he'd been taught all his life. However, tonight, he found that he didn't give a shit about how things looked. Let the town of Catfish Creek chatter, he was done taking shit from this man.

"Sir." Drew stood, closing his citation booklet. "I'm gonna have to take you in."

"On what charges?" Betty Sue asked, already reaching for her phone—no doubt to call their attorney.

"Possession of illegal fireworks and cruelty to animals for a start." Too bad general dumbassery and being a pain in the ass were constitutionally protected.

Beauford shot off the couch, faster than his arthritic knees probably appreciated. "You can't do that, I'm the mayor!"

There it was, the same veiled threat he'd heard a million times since he'd become sheriff. Friday couldn't come soon enough. He was sick and tired of the Groundhog Day his life had become.

He shrugged and grabbed the handcuffs hooked to his belt, not that he would use them on an old man but he couldn't wait to see Beauford's reaction. "What are you gonna do, have my job?"

"I know about Fort Worth, boy. Put those things on me and you can kiss that job goodbye right now."

Okay, now he *was* gonna put the bracelets on a seventy-six-year-old man. It might not be his proudest moment, but it was going to be one he'd remember fondly for the rest of his life.

He let the joy of that fill his face. "Guess that means I'll just have to shake things up a bit then."

Maybe he'd even look into getting a winter coat and a pair of snow boots.

Leah

Leah had just settled in on the couch to binge watch some trashy reality TV when someone knocked on the door. That was Catfish Creek, mid-sized city with a small town feel. It was probably a recently divorced neighbor with a casserole for the single sheriff or a group from a local church here to save his soul—either way, they were bound to be disappointed when he failed to answer.

Remembering the promise she made to Drew, she tiptoed up to the door and peered through the peephole. Curtis stood on the front porch in his now slightly wrinkled suit. His sunglasses were cockeyed and, judging by the tension in his jaw, he wasn't too happy about it.

"You know when you do that, the peephole goes dark," Curtis said. "Let me in."

Busted.

She cracked open the door, keeping one foot planted behind it. "What's up?"

"Nothing, just need to do a house check." He took a step forward, jerking to an awkward stop and narrowing his eyes at her when she didn't open the door wider to let him in.

"Drew already did that."

Curtis shrugged and put his hand on the door, not pushing against it but letting his intentions be known. "It's standard procedure."

The little hairs on the back of her neck tingled. Something was off. "I'm gonna call Drew."

She reached for the phone in the back pocket of her jeans at the same time as she started to shut the door. Curtis jabbed one of his scuffed-up size-twelve dress shoes into the opening.

"That's not how this is going to work." The door came flying open, sending Leah stumbling back. "Mr. Law wants his diamond."

Oh fuck.

Adrenaline shot through her veins making her twice as

fast as she sprinted toward the bedroom and the locked door that could give her the extra five seconds she needed to call 911. Curtis roared his displeasure and thundered after her. She made it as far as the hall closet when Curtis fisted her ponytail and she went flying backward.

"You're not going anywhere but with me, bitch."

She landed with a hard thunk against the floor. The phone bobbled in her grip as she fought to hold on to it before it went flying. Blood pounding in her ears, her fight response took over. Curtis had a hundred pounds and actual training going for him but she was out of fucks to give. She knew going with him meant only bad things. She came up screaming, putting everything into her punch. Her knuckles crashed into Curtis's nose. The bone cracked and blood streamed down over his lips that were curled into a grimace.

"Fucking bitch," he yelled and backhanded her hard.

Pain exploded in her cheekbone, rocking her back on her heels. She gripped her phone, her fingers connecting with her contacts list. Curtis's follow up punch landed just under her chin. The world was going dark before her head bounced against the floor. The last thing she heard before everything went dark was Tamara's voice, but it sounded a million miles away.

"B-Squad Investigations and Security, how can I help you?"

Drew

Drew couldn't stop smiling, not even when he was filling out arrest paperwork in the sheriff's office long after Beauford had posted bond, thanks to an expedited hearing courtesy of the mayor's poker buddy, Judge Harper. It would be decades before he ever forgot the look on the old man's face when he clicked the handcuffs around his wrists—if even then. Today was definitely a win.

"Sheriff, your cell keeps ringing," Deputy Lance Pepper called out.

Glancing out his office door, he saw the lanky new recruit walking toward him holding up Drew's cell. Damn. He'd forgotten it on the intake desk when he'd brought in Beauford. If it was one of the FBI agents calling to let him know Leah had slipped the nest, he was going to have to knock heads.

He took the cell from Pepper and swiped accept call. "Jackson here."

"Tell me she's with you," a woman said.

It took half a second to place the voice. It was Leah's B-Squad friend, Lexie. His gut clenched. "What's wrong?"

"Just answer the question dammit."

He grabbed his keys and headed for the door, leaving the half-finished paperwork laying on his desk. "She's at my house. The place is secured and there's an FBI agent parked out front."

"Tell me it's not Curtis."

Icy dread made him quicken his step. "What in the fuck is going on?"

"God, how to put this in laymen's terms," she said with a groan. "Okay, I used my *skills* to put a kind of secret Google alert on the systems I accessed so they'd alert when anyone connected with the diamond was mentioned. It went off right before we got the call from Leah's cell. Curtis is dirty. He's under investigation and he's gone dark."

He was out of the sheriff's office and halfway to his truck

before she'd gotten to the last word. "What do you mean got the call? What did she say?"

"Nothing."

He yanked his truck door open and vaulted inside. "What do you mean *nothing*?"

"No one was there. Everyone but Isaac and Tamara blew it off as a butt dial even though she didn't answer when Isaac called back. I just figured you two were getting it on like crazy sex monkeys."

He sped out of the lot, tires squealing. "When did this happen?"

"An hour ago," Lexie said in that calm voice only used by people who were scared shitless and refusing to acknowledge it. "Isaac and Tamara are in the chopper now. They'll be there in thirty minutes."

Half an hour wasn't a lot of time in the big picture but it sure as fuck sounded like forever as he blew threw a red light and slammed the gas pedal to the floor. Every cop knew that each minute counted in a situation like this. Still, he couldn't give in to the fear shoving his balls into his throat. He had to let his training take over, mentally distance himself. If he couldn't, things could go very wrong, very fast. He eased his foot off the gas and took the corner onto his street on all four wheels instead of two.

Forcing himself to release the breath he'd been holding, if not the fear gripping his gut, he slid into cop mode. "I'll call with an update as soon as I evaluate the scene at the house."

"Gotcha," Lexie paused, "and Drew?"

"Yeah?"

"It's gonna be alright. Leah's a fighter."

He was counting on it.

Confirmation of just how much of a fighter she was

came ten minutes later when he walked through the banged
up front door to his house. His living room looked like the
saloon in an old Western after a bar fight. Furniture was
turned over. Pictures that had been on the shelves were on
the floor in pieces. Shit was tossed everywhere. Worst of all,
Leah's Doc Marten boots were abandoned in the middle of
the mess. The woman herself was nowhere to be found.
What *was* in his house was a bright yellow Post-it note stuck
to his TV that read: 555-438-6821.

He grabbed his phone, but instead of dialing that
number he called the B-Squad office and had Lexie patch
him through to Isaac.

"They have her," he said by way of greeting.

"Motherfuckers," Isaac yelled over the sound of the helicopter. "So what's the plan?"

Drew took another look at that Post-it note and certainty
settled over him as tangible as armor. "I'm going to make
sure they live to regret this and if even a single hair on
Leah's head is hurt, I'm not gonna concern myself with the
living part."

Leah

Warren Law did not look like Leah's mental image of the
head of an international jewelry theft ring. He wore pleated
Dockers and a pressed golf shirt. If this were a movie, he'd
be the unassuming friend who was actually the heroine's
insane stalker because she'd had the audacity to turn him
down for sex and his fragile male ego had been harmed. He
was a total nice-guy-asshole type.

Warren stopped in front of the kitchen chair she was

tied to and peered down at her. She had to make quite the picture since she was Duct taped to the chair, had a length of the silver tape across her mouth and her left cheek was so swollen she could see the edge of it in her peripheral vision. If she could have flipped him off or snarled out a smart ass remark she would have. As it was, the best she could do was glare at him, which earned her a patronizing chuckle.

Warren patted her on the head and turned back to the shitbag of a dirty FBI agent. "I'm beginning to think she's not that important to him."

"She is," Curtis said, his voice sounding funny since he'd stuffed gauze up his broken nose.

Warren went stiff. "Are you telling me I'm wrong?"

"No, sir." Curtis's gaze dropped to the floor and he took a step back from the other man. "It's just, you haven't seen the two of them together. It's like they're an old married couple who still bang on the regular."

"How eloquent," Warren said.

That was one word for it. Leah would have chosen bull-shit. She hated Drew Jackson. It was just she couldn't help herself from stripping him naked—or wanting to—every time she was within sixty miles of him. That didn't mean anything. Sure, she'd grown up crushing on him and that summer he'd become her first love, but that was over. The feeling had flipped. Love and hate were opposite sides of the same coin, not the same thing at all.

Curtis shrugged. "You don't pay me to talk pretty."

"True." Warren nodded. "I pay you for the information you can provide about what the FBI is up to. Now that is no more."

Oh, he sounded pissed. Looked like someone wasn't going to get a good employee review come bonus time.

"They knew," Curtis said. "It's why I had to get rid of Ritter. He'd been informing on me."

Got rid of. You didn't have to be a scumbag to know what that meant. Fuck. All of the sass drained right out of her.

"You do realize you didn't tape over her ears too?" Warren asked, jerking her chin toward Leah.

Nope. She wasn't here. Not really. The ringing in her ears from being knocked out was too loud for her to hear anything. Surely, if she thought it loud enough they'd hear it.

Curtis turned and looked at her, his hand going to his swollen nose. "Is she really getting out of here?"

"No, I guess not," Warren said.

The urge to panic and fight against her bonds was nearly overwhelming, but she'd already gone that route when she'd woken up and found herself in the shitty kitchenette. It hadn't helped.

"Everything with this heist has gone wrong, my cover is blown, and now I'm stuck clipping all the loose ends," Warren said, grimacing. "The good news though is after I move this damned diamond, I'm going to disappear to someplace tropical for a good long while."

Warren's phone rang out a hard rock anthem. Everyone stilled. Warren glanced down at the phone, his smile sent a shiver down her spine.

"Sheriff, I'd begun to think you didn't care," Warren said before pausing, an amused expression on his face. "You have a real talent for language. I've never been threatened quite like that before and believe me, in this line of work, being threatened is du rigor. However, we're not here for a friendly chat. We'll make the exchange tomorrow at high noon. Bring the diamond to the high school gym." He waited while Drew said something Leah couldn't make out. "Yes, I'm aware it will be crowded, what with all the last minute preparations for the reunion tomorrow. This place really goes all out for that sort of thing, don't they?" She couldn't understand the words Drew used in response but the pissed off tone was unmistakable. "I suppose you don't give a shit about the reunion preparations. I hope that attitude doesn't carry over to sweet Leah here. I'd hate to be disappointed." Without waiting for Drew to say anything else, Warren hung up and slid the phone in the front pocket of his pleated Dockers, walked over to the kitchen counter and slid open one of the drawers.

"All set?" Curtis asked.

"Almost." He took something out of the drawer and spun around, something black and metal in his hand.

She had a second to register the handgun with a silencer attached before the muffled shot boomed in her ears, a million times louder than it was in reality. Curtis went down but left half of his head on the wall behind him.

"I'm not normally a violent man," Warren said, his voice cold. "But loose ends are meant to be tied"

Leah couldn't breathe. Couldn't think. Panic roared in her ears. She yanked at the Duct taped bonds securing her forearms to the chair with all her strength and tugged at the ones holding her calves to the chair legs. By the time the fear and adrenaline had abated enough for her to think any single thought beyond "get out" she realized Warren had disappeared down the hall leading away from the kitchen, leaving her alone with the dead man and her terrified thoughts.

8

Drew

There was no way in hell Drew was waiting until tomorrow to rescue Leah. That little lie had only been to buy some time and make Law feel like he was in control. In reality, Drew and Lexie had kicked it into high gear. He'd pulled rank for the last time in Catfish Creek and the sheriff's office SWAT was on its way. By the time Isaac and Tamara got to his house, it would be go time.

He set down his night scope next to the rest of the weapons he'd gathered. The surface of his kitchen table was invisible under the armory spread out on it. Overkill? Hopefully, but he wasn't going to chance Leah's safety on being short a box of bullets. The thought made bile rise in his throat. Focusing on the job had been the only thing keeping him sane since he'd gotten off the phone with Law. He—scratch that—Leah couldn't afford for him to surrender to the what-ifs and could-happens.

He glanced down at his cell sitting in the middle of the weapons. "Lexie, tell me you've found something."

"I've narrowed it down to two possibilities," the hacker's voice crackled out of his cell phone's crappy speaker.

His gut clenched. "Possibilities? I thought you were good."

"Fuck you very much, I'm amazing but I can't magic people out of thin air."

Shit.

He dialed back the anxiety again. "You're right. I'm sorry."

"Don't worry about it. I'm not feeling very polite right now either," she said. "Okay, the first is one of those communal living buildings developers are pushing on the young and dumb."

Communal living? "I don't even know what that means."

"It's like a dorm but for adults," she explained. "The unit in Catfish Creek has individual studio apartments and a few one-bedroom units with kitchenettes."

"What makes you think they're there?"

"A combination of red-light camera video showing Curtis's government-issued car at different locations nearby and security footage from an ATM across the street that showed a man and a woman fitting Curtis's and Leah's descriptions going inside."

All of that sounded like a lock. The fact that it wasn't had him pacing across his kitchen's tile floor. "I hear a but."

Lexie let out a tortured sigh, obviously as wound up as he was. "The lighting in the video sucked and the angle was worse. It could be Curtis holding up a wobbly Leah or it could be a drunk couple weaving their way home after a long night."

Fuck. Not what he wanted to hear. "Option two?"

"An extended-stay hotel a mile away from the first possibility."

"What makes it look good for this?" he asked as he grabbed the phone and carried it to the darkened living room where he could watch the street for activity without being observed.

"The location and the fact that someone is registered under an alias Law uses."

"Why isn't that a for sure?" Jesus, the woman liked to draw things out.

"Because John Smith is one of the favorite alias' of cheating husbands too. If it is him, it's a brilliantly stupid move."

If he'd been in a more charitable mood and not on the verge of killing the asshole, Drew would have agreed.

"Isaac and Tamara there yet?" Lexie asked. "I'm showing they should be."

A set of headlights appeared on his darkened street. A second later, a nondescript car pulled into his drive. Isaac and an icy blonde got out.

"They're here."

"Good. I'm shooting you the addresses and building layout specs of each target right now," Lexie said. "Bring her home."

As if failure was even an option.

"I'll be doing that," he said. "No matter what."

Leah

The kitchen was pitch dark, but the metallic scent of fresh blood penciled in every detail she couldn't see of Curtis's dead body only a few feet from her. This wasn't a place she ever saw herself going. If she was going to die in Catfish

Creek, she'd always figured it would have been one of The Hamburger Shack greasy burgers that would do her in. The panicked giggle that escaped was muffled by the Duct tape across her mouth.

She tested the tape securing her forearm to the chair. Despite her pulling, tugging, and yanking, it hadn't budged.

There was no way Warren was going to let her or anyone else walk away tomorrow even if he got the diamond—his killing Curtis without even blinking showed just how far over the line Warren had gone. There was no coming back. And if she didn't do something, he'd take out Drew. She wouldn't—couldn't—let that happen. Even the thought of it made all the air disappear from the room and there was only one explanation for that, the kind you came to when you could count the rest of your life in minutes and everything else that seemed so important before slipped away.

For someone who's supposed to be a brainiac, you sure can be stupid.

She loved Drew. She'd loved him since she was six years old and as much as he'd broken her heart, all the jagged pieces were still meant for only one man and she wasn't about to let some psycho hurt him.

Drew

The deputies in the unmarked mobile command unit were four blocks down. Drew stood at the halfway point between Lexie's top two possibilities and right in the middle of Isaac Camacho's glare zone. The fuck yous had gone unspoken so far. As former military special forces, Isaac knew as well as Drew did that they didn't have time for that now. Later?

They'd probably both walk away with black eyes and bruises—but just because Drew knew he deserved them didn't mean he was going to take his medicine without hitting back.

"I don't like splitting up," Isaac grumbled, shoving a hand through his shaggy brown hair.

"Too bad," Drew said. "We have two possible locations and one could simply be a decoy. We can't take that chance with Leah's life on the line."

Isaac puffed up his chest and took a step toward him. "Wonder who in the hell let that happen."

Pound for pound, inch for inch they were evenly matched. Add to that the fact that they were both pissed off at the same person and it could go explosive fast.

"It's not the time or the place," Tamara said, a harsh enough blast of frigid cold in her tone to stop Drew in his tracks.

"You're right." Drew nodded at the woman who looked every inch like the bitchy ex-beauty queen she was. "Won't happen again."

"Oh yes it will," Isaac countered. "But not until after we have my sister back."

"Then let's get to it. We're all patched into the SWAT command center." He tapped the communicator that looked like an earbud but worked for ingoing and outgoing voice traffic, not to mention the ability to go old school and talk in tapped code to communicate when talking wasn't an option. "You take the communal living place and I'll check out the extended stay hotel."

"What, no backup?" Isaac asked with a snarl.

Already amped up, Drew reached deep for the calm he needed to get through this. "I can handle it. Anyway, my extra guys are out looking for the other FBI agent, Ritter, and manning the command center so this doesn't go pear shaped. This is Catfish Creek, in case you forgot it, it's not like we've got an unending supply of deputies."

After a curt nod from Isaac, Drew continued. "Anyway, it's recon only. When we locate her, we call in the others before attempting to exfil. Are we clear?"

Isaac nodded. "Crystal."

With a nod, he took off at a jog, sticking close to the shadows toward the Metroplex Extended Stay Hotel. John Smith was staying in room four eighteen. There wasn't anyone in the rooms above, below or beside him, according to what Lexie was able to bring up—all of which made his gut twitch considering how hard it was to get a hotel room in Catfish Creek this week.

Getting through the front door of the hotel when he was in full black tactical clothing, wearing a bulletproof vest, and carrying enough firepower to take out the building got him a panicked look from the hotel clerk. He stopped long enough to show his badge and to warn the clerk to stay low and safe if trouble came her way. Then he was sprinting up four flights of stairs, his only mental image that of Leah like he'd last seen her with that smart ass smile that twisted him up inside. Picturing her any other way could fuck up his ability to get the job done.

Still breathing steady he walked through the stairwell door and out into the carpeted hallway that would muffle his steps as he approached the door for room four eighteen.

He fished out the reverse scope from his gear bag and lined it up on the door's peephole. All he saw was black. Not a solid black as if someone had taped over the peephole but some serious darkness. Willing himself not to jump the gun and pick the door lock before he knew the situation, he stared through the scope trying to pick out any variations in lighting. Just as he was about to give up and pop the door lock, a soft beam of light appeared, drawing his attention. The light silhouetted a man with a medium build but that wasn't what made his blood freeze in his veins. It was the unmistakable splatter of gray matter on the wall of a kitchenette and Leah Duct taped to a chair.

On the inhale he tapped out the target-located signal for the deputies in the mobile command unit and on the exhale the heel of his boot was slamming into the door near the lock, sending it flying open.

Leah

As soon as the light went on and the sound of Warren walking down the short hall reached Leah, a calmness settled through her. She'd worked it out already. Controlling her, grabbing the diamond, and getting away was a helluva lot harder as a one-man band then if Warren had still had his toady, Curtis. There was no way he'd take her to the exchange. More than likely he'd give some story about her being at a secondary location. Maybe she would be, she just wouldn't be there and breathing.

Despite her attempts to escape, she was still bound to the chair. There hadn't been enough time.

She raised her chin and let her face go blank. If she was going out, it wasn't going to be while begging. Instead, she'd hold on to the one thing that had gotten her this far, the realization that she hadn't ever really come back to Catfish Creek just to see the now-bedraggled cheerleaders or for the reunion at all. She'd come for Drew. And she'd gotten to be with him one last time. That was ending things on a high note.

"Oh the stench is killing me," Warren said, stopping a few feet away from Curtis's body. "I'm afraid we need to expedite our timeline."

Before she could even think of a smart remark to serve as her final words, the door flew open and crashed against the wall.

"Hands where I can see them," Drew shouted.

Dressed in all black with his face grim and his gun drawn, he looked every bit like an avenging demon bent on destruction.

"There's no reason for such viole—" Warren said, one hand up and the other sneaking around his back.

She screamed through the Duct tape covering her mouth, trying to warn him.

"Move that hand any way but skyward and I'm gonna blow your head off," Drew said, sounding every bit like a man who'd welcome the opportunity to pull the trigger.

Warren hesitated, his gaze jumping from Drew in the door to the windows and back again, then slowly raised his other hand. Drew didn't even look her way as he marched across the bloodied kitchenette and took the gun from where Warren had tucked it in his waistband.

"Down on the ground, fingers interlocked behind your head."

Warren did what he was told. Drew shoved a foot down between Warren's shoulder blades and only then did Drew glance up at her. The furious darkness in his eyes made her breath catch.

"Are you okay?" he asked, the muscle in his jaw twitching.

Unable to talk or run to him, she nodded. He'd come for

her. How in the hell he'd found her, she had no idea, but he had. Relief seeped through her as she looked at the man she loved, wishing like hell she could just tell him.

A heartbeat later though and it was chaos in the cramped kitchenette as deputies, paramedics, and her brother swarmed inside. Before she could say anything to Drew, Isaac herded her outside and to the waiting ambulance.

The entire time the paramedic poked, prodded and shined a light in her eyes, Leah kept an eye out for Drew, but he never appeared.

"Ma'am, we're gonna need to take you in so the docs can check you out."

She shook her head, trying her best to force the throb in her head from Curtis's knock out punch to stop. "I'll go later, I want to talk to Drew."

Isaac crossed his arms and stepped directly into her line of sight until his broad chest was all she could see. "You'll go now nicely, or I'll haul your ass there kicking and screaming."

Isaac was usually the most easy-going of the Camachos, right up until he wasn't anymore. That was probably what happened when you grew up with five strong-willed sisters and a single mom who ruled with an iron fist. Isaac bent, but he never, ever broke—and, judging by the stubborn look on his face, he wasn't giving in this time.

"Can you let him know where I'm going?" she asked.

Her brother's only response was to glare at her. She glared right back, even if it did make her head ache.

"Good Lord, you two." Tamara rolled her eyes. "I'll tell him, Leah, go on to the hospital. We'll be following right behind the ambulance."

Knowing they were right—especially when her head felt

like someone had crashed two bricks on either side of it—she nodded her agreement. Isaac and the paramedic had the ambulance doors shut before she got a chance to change her mind.

Isaac

There were two things you did not fuck with when it came to Isaac Camacho. His truck and the women in his life—and definitely *not* in that order. He stood outside the doors of the hospital ER and waited, silent and still in the entranceway's shadows. Drew would be here sooner rather than later and he was going to have to go through Isaac to get inside. He didn't give a flying fuck if the other man was the Catfish Creek Sheriff or the President of the United States, he was going to pay the price for putting Leah in danger.

"You can't break him," Tamara said from her spot beside him. She'd been out here with him since the docs took Leah behind closed doors again to try to talk her into staying the night for observation or at least getting a CT scan.

"Why not?" he asked, already jonsing for the opportunity to dole out some big brother justice.

"He loves her."

No. He loved his sister. Drew just fucked with her head. "What makes you say that?"

"I have eyeballs, an amazing brain, and I've seen you in a similar state," she said with a grin.

Isaac turned to look his fiancée up and down. It wasn't a hardship. Tall, blonde, and so pretty it made his body ache. She also had a tart personality and a brain that moved faster than his own, two things that had transformed raw lust into solid love not that long ago.

"What state is that, darlin'?"

She grinned and shook her head. "Desperate and between a rock and a hard place."

He stiffened. "What happened with us was different."

"Really?" she asked, all false innocence and sweetness he didn't believe for a second. "You mean you didn't move heaven and earth to get to me when my crazy ass cult leader brother-in-law lost his mind, held me hostage, and tried to marry his sixteen-year-old daughter to one of his middle-aged followers?"

Acid burned its way up his gullet at the memory of the worst fucking day of his entire life. "You know I did."

"And Drew must have broken about a thousand standard operating procedures, rules and regulations to get to Leah tonight," Tamara said, snuggling in next to him.

The feel of her mouthwatering curves momentarily distracted him and he forgot for a second what they were talking about. "What are you trying to say?"

"Take your punch if you need to, but don't break him or you'll face Leah's wrath."

A flush of anger burned its way up from his toes tucked into his cowboy boots. Oh yeah. Drew Jackson. The prick who almost got his sister killed. "Her crush on him was kid stuff. She's beyond over that."

Tamara snorted her disbelief. "How did someone so clueless manage to hook a hottie like me?"

It was a question he'd wondered himself often enough that he had the perfect comeback—one that was also damn close to the truth if not the whole truth. "My big dick and all the fabulous things I can do with it."

"Yep, when you're not acting like one, that prick of yours

is very nice to have around." Letting her fingers trail up his thigh as she leaned in, she brushed her lips across his in a quick kiss. A set of high-set headlights lit up the dark corner where they stood. She broke contact and looked toward the truck parking near the entrance. "Remember, be nice."

A quick, hard smack on his ass later and Tamara sashayed through the ER's automatic doors. The woman was mean as hell when she wanted to be, but she was also usually right. If he didn't love her so damned much, that fact would probably annoy the hell out of him.

Drew hustled across the parking lot and stopped in front of Isaac. "How is she?"

He debated lying just to mess with the other man's head, but decided against it when he spotted the tortured shadows in his eyes. Isaac knew that look, the one when bad shit happened because he'd fucked up, because he'd worn it himself. He couldn't jerk the guy around when he look like that. "The docs say she'll be fine but they want to do a CT scan because of the probable concussion."

"What does she say to that?" Drew rubbed his palm across the back of his neck hard enough to take off a few layers of skin.

Isaac chuckled. "Lots of colorful words our mama would not approve of."

"Sounds about right." Drew grinned, but it only lasted a second. "So is now when you try to knock me on my ass?"

It should be. But instead of hammering the dude, he remembered what Tamara said. Love? Judging by the way Drew looked, it could be. So instead of curling his hands into fists, he asked a question. "Do I have a reason to?"

"Yeah, you do." No excuses. No whining. Just regret.

"Why's that?"

Drew's whole body went stiff and fury sparked in his

eyes. "She could have been killed because I failed to protect her."

"We're professionals at this," Isaac said, offering Drew an opportunity to walk away and save face. "We both know shit goes sideways sometimes."

"It shouldn't have with her," he said with an angry growl. "*Never* with her."

"Fuck. Tamara is right again." Isaac almost laughed out loud at the sudden confused look on Drew's face. Man, he hated to enlighten the guy—especially since it was his sister they were talking about—but someone had to and if Drew took it anywhere near as hard as Isaac had, it would hit harder than a fist ever could. "You love her."

"Tamara?" Drew asked, obviously not following along.

All the amusement drained out of Isaac's body. "Not unless you want to die slow, you moron. Leah. You're in love with Leah."

Drew didn't respond. He just stood there and glowered, his hands curled into tight fists at his side. Jesus. The man had it bad. It almost made Isaac feel bad about what had to happen next, but not enough to change plans. Balancing on the balls of his feet, he exhaled and swung his right fist at three-quarters strength connecting with Drew's cheek and sending the other man stumbling back a couple of steps.

Eyes bleeding the kind of amped-up tension that always blazed to the surface after a mission, Drew rubbed his face and shot him a dirty look. "You asshole."

Isaac shrugged, being sure to stay on guard even as his stance said nothing but good old Texas boy fun. "I've been accused of worse."

Drew launched himself at Isaac, landing an uppercut that made his teeth clang together and knocked him off balance. It was a nice shot that was gonna hurt in the morning. The other man followed through by wrapping his arms around him football style and taking him down like he was a tackling dummy at the start of two-a-days. After that it was just a series of half assed jabs and the occasional well-placed punch as they rolled on the small grassy area off to the left of the ER entrance.

"What in the hell is wrong with the both of you?" Leah's shouted question made Isaac's ears ring more than Drew's punch.

Shit. She sounded *exactly* like mom. The shock of it hit him so hard that he didn't dodge in time to miss Drew's final punch to his gut and all the air wheezed out of him. As he tried to get air back in his lungs, he glanced over at the ER doors where Leah stood with Tamara. Neither of them looked very impressed with either him or Drew at the moment.

"Lucky shot, dickface," he managed to get out when he could suck in a breath.

Drew didn't pay him any mind.

"Are you two done because I could really use someone who will wait with me until it's time to do the CT scan," Leah said. "The doc and Tessa talked me into it."

Thank God for Tessa Daniels, the cardiac nurse Leah had gone to high school with who'd spent her break in the ER giving his sister the what for about trying to skip out on a CT at the very least.

"I'll do it," he and Drew said at the same time, both of them scrambling up from the grass.

"Can you manage it without taking another swing at each other?" Tamara asked, arms crossed and hip jutting out.

"I'm good." Oh hell, that was definitely her don't-fuck-with-me stance. Isaac turned to Drew. "You good?"

"Yeah." Drew nodded as he used his thumb to wipe away the blood at the corner of his mouth.

Like a man with only one purpose in life, he strode over to Leah. They didn't touch. They didn't have to. It was awkward just watching them look at each other as if they were having an entire conversation and then going inside without ever saying a word.

"Was all of that really necessary?" Tamara asked when he reached her side.

"Yeah." Nothing gave away a man's intentions more than a couple of rounds in the ring—or on the grass depending on the circumstances.

"Are you satisfied that I'm right?" She hooked her arm through his as they walked toward the ER doors. "Come on, I want to hear it."

That was his Tamara. She never gave up. Ever. "You're right."

"I know that hurt to say." She brushed her lips across his already bruising cheek. "Let's get in there before Leah changes her mind about the CT."

9

Leah

The rest of the hospital was a blur. In the beginning it felt like so much sit and wait, but by the end it was all hurrying from one spot to another until the doctors confirmed she didn't have a concussion and sent her on her way. That didn't mean she was totally off the hook, of course. She had to agree not to be by herself for the next twelve hours and she needed to be woken up every few hours tonight to make sure her condition hadn't changed. After that there was some more dick measuring between Isaac and Drew until she told them both to go take a flying leap and that she was going where her bags were and that meant Drew's house. That was her story anyway. The truth, she only admitted to herself when Drew pulled into his garage, hustled around to the passenger side, and helped her out before leading her into the kitchen.

One touch from him and she was home, safe with the man she loved. After everything that had happened tonight she wasn't going to ask why, she was just going with what she knew in her gut was right—and that was being with him. He went into the house first, tension clear in the unforgiving lines of his shoulders and the hard edge to his jaw. He was just as tuned up as she was, heat and a dangerous volatility emanated from him in waves.

"I gotta warn you," he said, positioning his body so it blocked her line of sight. "The living room's still a mess."

She flinched and her hand flew to her swollen cheek, not meaning to but unable to help it. Drew's arms were around her before her brain registered her reaction to the mention of the room where she'd fought and lost to Curtis.

"I'm sorry," he said, his words brushing against her hair. "We can go somewhere else."

That was the last thing she wanted. The need to touch and be touched, to confirm everything was alright, that normally came after a serious adrenaline rush was compounded by the fact that she was with Drew.

She shook her head and tilted her face up. "I'm not planning on spending time in the living room tonight anyway."

He looked down at her, his gaze zeroing in on her mouth. His pupils dilated and his nostrils flared with a lust that her body recognized at once. Her nipples puckered and her body hummed with need so strong she had to clench her thighs together.

But just as fast as it appeared, he blinked the desire away and a neutral mask slid onto his face. "Yeah, you should rest up."

Oh no, he wasn't going to shut them down tonight. "Don't wanna do that either."

He glanced over at the fridge as the vein in his temple worked at a frantic pace. "Snack?"

"What's wrong, Drew?" She stepped closer and ran her

hands across the soft cotton of his T-shirt, relishing all the hard muscle laying underneath. "Nervous all the sudden?"

He grimaced and looked toward the ceiling as if he'd find answers there or was praying for strength. "You just got out of the hospital."

"Where they said I was perfectly okay." She dropped her hands to the buttons of his black tactical pants.

He captured both of her wrists in one hand, stopping her before she could make more progress. "You have to be woken up every two to three hours."

"Then it's a good thing I know the perfect way to stay awake."

Not bothering to try to break his hold, she raised herself up on her tiptoes, relishing the heat of his body against hers, the musky male scent of his skin, and the solid reassurance of his strong body. Then she gave in to temptation and brushed her lips up the line of his throat to the stubble along his jawline.

He let out a tortured groan that only encouraged her.

"I don't know that we should. You've had a rough night."

"It was doctor's orders." She nipped at his bottom lip. "And I know how much you love to follow the rules."

"Really? When I'm around you, it seems like all I do is break them."

He lowered his head and she knew she had him. She leaned in and kissed him, her tongue sweeping across his juicy bottom lip before sweeping inside. He groaned his appreciation, a low, bass sound that reverberated through him, and released her wrists. His hands went straight to her ass and he lifted her so she fit snug and tight against his hard cock that was straining against his pants. Desire made her chest tight and her muscles loose.

"Take me to your bed and fuck me senseless, Drew Jackson."

"You need this cock, Sweets?"

She ground against his hard length, desperate for him-- not just his body but the man himself. She loved him, had always loved him, and he was the only one who could give her what she needed. "So fucking bad that it hurts."

"Don't worry, I'll give it to you." He carried her out of the kitchen. "I'll always give you what you want."

Drew

Drew laid her gently on his bed. This was the last thing they should be doing, but he had to touch her to confirm to himself that she was here and okay. And with her looking at him with those big eyes and a green and purple bruise trying to take over one side of her face there was no way he could tell her no when she needed the same thing as much as he did.

As much as it killed him, he would go slow, tender, and only as much as she needed. "Tell me what you need."

She sat up, her hands going to his pants again. "You." With deft fingers and a hungry look in her eyes, she popped the button and slid down the zipper. "Hard and fast."

The wet tip of his aching cock poked through the opening in his boxers and she dipped her head down, lapping at the pre-come on the swollen head. A white bolt of pleasure shot through him that made his lungs seize. He clenched his hands into fists as he fought to maintain some kind of control over his body's reaction.

"Sweets." It came out half prayer and half plea. "We should take it slow."

"Fuck that." She reached up and shoved his pants and boxers down. "I need you." She wrapped her fingers around his concrete dick and stroked it with the kind of tight pressure that made his eyes roll back in his head. "I need you filling me up until I can't take anymore."

When his sight returned a second later, Leah was staring up at him with his dick in her hand and his resistance blew away like tumbleweeds in a windstorm. There was no going back. He loved her. Loved every maddening thing about her. Tonight he'd almost lost her.

He cupped her face and tilted it up toward him. "So good you won't ever be able to forget."

"I never can with you." She turned her head and kissed the inside of his palm and then, because it was Leah, she sucked one of his fingers into his mouth.

All of the blood in his brain went south in a rush. Later he'd tell her how he felt, but now he needed to show her.

"Get your clothes off."

"Is that how we're doing this?" She dropped her hands to the hem of her shirt and whipped it off over her head revealing another hot pink bra. "With you ordering me around?"

"You get off on it." And God knew so did he.

She grinned and undid her jeans. "I do."

Quick as lightning, he bent down and grabbed her ankles, sending her backwards so she was flat on her back on his bed. He yanked her jeans off in one fluid motion, releasing her long legs and a pair of hot pink panties so small they barely qualified as underwear. The sight was enough to make his mouth go dry. Then he spotted the damp center of her panties and his balls tightened.

Slow and gentle? Yeah. That wasn't going to happen.

"Take them off before I rip them off," he ordered.

Without asking any questions, she hooked her fingers into the elastic waistband and slid them down her hips before lifting her legs so her toes were pointed at the ceiling. "Help a girl out?"

He didn't need to be asked twice. He whipped them up her legs and tossed them to the floor.

"Spread them. Let me see what's mine."

Keeping her legs skyward she did just that until her legs formed the perfect V with her juicy pussy at its apex. It was pink and wet and the only place in the world he wanted to be. He kicked off his shoes and got rid of the rest of his clothes in record time.

"Damn, you're so wet for me." He skimmed the pad of his thumb down her slick folds, rewarded by the way her thighs shook the moment he touched her. "I was going to make you wait and beg to feel this big cock in you." He slid his thumb inside, rubbing against the sensitive skin on the bottom of her opening as he did so. She moaned, dropped her legs so her feet were planted on the bed, and lifted her hips to take in more of him. "You have a hungry little pussy though, don't you, Sweets?" One, two, three pumps of his thumb inside her as she rocked her body against him. "It would be cruel to deny you." He withdrew his thumb and then circled it around her hard clit before leaning forward over her. "I want to taste you so bad, but I know you need cock."

"Now," she said, leaning up enough to reach behind her, unhook her bra, and toss it away.

That was his Leah. Beautiful. Demanding. Ballsy enough to go after what she wanted, no matter what. "Then open your mouth and don't suck."

Anticipation sparkled in her eyes as she complied.

He slid his thumb, wet with her desire, over her ruby red mouth. "Don't you dare lick that off." Faster than he'd ever moved before, he reached over and grabbed a condom from the drawer of his bedside table and rolled it on. His balls were already tight against his body and his dick was hot and ready to blow and he hadn't even sunk inside her tight walls yet. Tormenting them both wasn't smart, but he couldn't seem to help it. He glided the tip of his cock over her clit, loving the way she moaned and writhed beneath him, and then lined up with her opening. Resisting the primal urge to surge forward, he leaned over her, her slick mouth only inches from his.

"Now I can taste you and fuck you at the same time." He crashed his mouth down onto hers at the same time as he pushed his hips forward and buried himself balls deep in her welcoming heat.

There was nothing slow or gentle about this. It wasn't like making love on a lazy Sunday afternoon. It was a desperate, almost crazy fuck—hard, demanding, and right on the edge of rough.

Leah's hands cupped his ass, her nails biting into his flesh as she pulled him forward and lifted her hips so he sank deeper inside her.

"God, yes," she cried out.

High on the taste and feel of her, he lifted his chest enough that he could look down at where their bodies joined.

"That's it, Sweets." Fuck. The image of his glistening wet cock plunging in and out of her was one he never wanted to forget. "God, I love watching your pussy swallow up my dick."

"Feels so good." She wrapped her legs tight around his waist, tipping her hips to deepen the angle. "So right."

"That's because it is. This is how it should be with us." He didn't mean the sex—although it was phenomenal—and he was pretty damn sure she didn't either. Whatever else happened, this wasn't over when she left Catfish Creek.

In and out, forward and back, he pounded into her as she met every thrust. The friction, the force, the tempo being exactly what was needed to take them both to the edge and push them right over. It started at the base of his spine--the tingling that built with each breath, each thrust, each time she undulated against him. He was close, so damn close but he couldn't come yet—not until he felt her squeeze him tight.

"Drew," she moaned, her head thrown back and her hips moving in tandem with his. "Faster. Please. So close."

"That's it, Sweets. Show me how bad that pussy wants this cock." He grabbed her hips and slid them both down the bed. Then, without ever leaving the heaven of her heat, he dropped his feet to the floor and stood up, lifting her hips as he did so their bodies lined up perfectly. "You're so tight. Squeeze that pussy for me. Milk that cock."

She reacted to his words just like he knew she would— grinding against him, pushing them both to go higher. He jerked her against him, going so deep his balls were wet with her juice. The vibrations in his spine increased and his ass clenched. It was too good. He wasn't going to make it much longer. He tightened his grasp on her hips, lifting her higher and speeding his pace while at the same time moving his thumb so he caressed her swollen clit.

The touch was all it took and she came around him, her entire body bowing as she cried out. In the face of such beauty there was no way he could hold back any longer. He barely recognized the sound of his own strangled groan as he climaxed with one final thrust deep within her.

Coming back to earth took a minute and he was still breathing hard when he got rid of the condom and collapsed on the bed next to her in a haze of post-coital satisfaction.

"You okay?" he asked, drawing her close to him as he yanked the covers over them.

"Better than just okay." She settled her cheek against the pocket of his shoulder. "How about you?"

"My brain is mush."

Her giggle tickled his chest. "That means we did it right."

"True," he said, squeezing her closer.

"So while I have you in this weakened state, I have a question for you."

"What's that?"

She drew lazy circles with her fingertip over his chest and down lower over his abs. His dick started to perk up in hopes of a little extra attention. Greedy fucker. Not that his brain, if it had been functioning at full strength, would have disagreed.

"Will you go to the reunion dance with me tomorrow night?" she asked.

He looked down at her, surprised by the nervousness he saw on her face. "Like a date?"

"Yeah." She tugged her bottom lip between her teeth. "Something new."

"I'd love to go." Okay, he had no interest in the reunion, especially when it wasn't even his graduating class, but if it meant getting to spend more time with Leah then he'd do just about anything. "So you never did tell me the real reason why you came back for the reunion."

"I came back," she said, her gaze steady even as her voice trembled a little, "for you."

Every dark fantasy he had about wringing the life out of

Warren Law evaporated with those five words. Something in his chest clicked into place. "Coming back to burn me alive or rescue me?"

"Am I allowed to say both?" she asked with a laugh.

God knew he deserved one more than the other. "You know, I've always regretted what an ass I was to you at the end of that summer. It's no excuse but I was young and dumb. I had no idea just how rare it is to find someone like you."

"You mean trouble?"

"A little of that but that's not all." Not by a long shot. How in the world it had taken him this long to figure it out was a testament to his own stupidity. "You're brave and smart and stubborn enough to stick to your guns when just about everyone was against you. I'm sorry for what happened with Jess in school. If it helps at all, she's changed since then. I think she realized that she wasn't turning into the kind of person she wants to be."

She brushed a kiss above his heart. "This town does weird stuff to us."

"It does have a tinge of crazy sticking to it." And that was putting it mildly.

"Ever think of leaving?"

"Only every day." And he'd finally figured out a destination. It wasn't Fort Worth and he wasn't sure how she'd react, so he kept his mouth shut.

"You know, Colorado is nice. It has four seasons and me. You should come visit sometime. You might like it enough to stay."

The hell yes was on the tip of his tongue but he swallowed it. Saying she'd had a rough day was putting it mildly. The last thing he wanted was to put any kind of pressure on her about them and what this could turn into—especially if this was all just post-orgasm-happy talk on her part. "How can I turn down an offer like that from a naked woman in my bed?"

"You don't." More lazy circles traced on his chest, but she couldn't hide the way her eyelids were drooping and the soft yawn that escaped her lips. "So what are you going to do come Monday when you're no longer sheriff?"

He glided his hand up and down her back as her eyes fluttered shut, too entranced to look away even for a second. "I'll figure out something."

"You always do," she said and gave in to the need for sleep.

Drew waited, listening to her deep breaths and promising himself that he would find a way to make it all work out. When he was sure she was deep asleep, he unwound himself from her and made his way to his laptop in the kitchen, determined to find a way to make that pledge come true.

10

Leah

The Catfish Creek High School had never looked so glam. The decorations that had looked like a bunch of mishmash Tuesday had come together into an elegant whole. There were gold chairs around circular tables, black and red decorations hanging from the walls, twinkle lights on the ceiling, and masks hanging down instead of balloons or streamers. The whole elegant effect was the last thing Leah expected—well, second to last. The absolute last thing she'd expected was to be teetering on the edge of forever with the man whose palm rested on the bare skin of her lower back as they stood just inside the gym doors.

"Don't tell me you're thinking of running now," Drew whispered in her ear, sending a shiver of desire down her spine.

"Not a chance."

"Good because that dance floor may be the only decent

excuse I've got to hold you as close as I need to right now. That dress is killing me."

She smoothed her hands down the clingy black dress with its conservative front and deep V cutout in the back that ended at the base of her spine. If he had any clue how small her pink panties had to be to not be seen above the cutout, they never would have made it out of his house. Add a pair of killer heels in her favorite shade of ebony and she was all legs, ass, and back—it was almost as if she'd packed it in her suitcase with Drew in mind.

"This old thing?" She tossed her hair back over one shoulder so it teased the bare skin between her shoulder blades and would have winked at him if it wasn't for the stupid masks they'd both been required to put on for entrance. "I only wear it when I don't care what I look like."

Linking her hand in his, she led Drew out onto the dance floor where couples in fancy outfits and detailed masks were swaying to a slow song. Despite the disguises, she recognized a few people in the gym. Gray and Tessa were there, both dancing with other people though. So was Jessica, with whom Drew shared a knowing look and a smile. He'd sworn last night that his sister wasn't the same person she had been. God knew leaving Catfish Creek behind had changed her, maybe it was time to give another Jackson a second chance. They'd been friends once, there wasn't any law that said because of a shitty high school experience they couldn't be again.

Before that thought could spiral into another though, Drew pulled her close and everyone else in the room disappeared. All she could see was him. It felt so right to be in his arms, but Leah couldn't quite settle the nerves making her stomach do the weird flip-flop thing it always did when she wasn't exactly sure what was going to happen next. This was usually when she ran or, at the very least, put on her bitchy bad girl attitude—but she refused to let herself do that tonight. Drew wasn't the only one breaking bad habits it seemed.

The song ended way before she was ready and they walked hand in hand to one of the tables.

"What can I get you from the bar?" he asked.

"Dr. Pepper, gotta get the good stuff while I'm still in Texas." It never tasted as good anywhere else.

"You got it." He dipped his head lower so his mouth was only inches from hers. "I just need a little something before I go." He closed the distance between them, pulling her body close at the same time that his tongue slid between her lips in a demanding kiss she was more than willing to surrender to.

Hot didn't begin to describe it, but face of the sun times two might come close as her body responded automatically to his touch. Warm, wet desire had her clenching her thighs together as she gave back as good as she got. Nothing else mattered at that moment but Drew. If he'd whispered in her ear for her to get on her knees she would have, her mouth open and wanting before she hit the gym floor. Luckily—or unluckily—he ended the kiss without anything more scandalous than making her nipples so hard she could get a second job etching glass. With a wink for her and a nod for the people sitting at the table, he turned and left for the bar while she tried to remember her name and why in the hell she was back home in Catfish Creek.

One look at the people sitting at her table, though, cleared the fog of lust in her brain in a hurry. Karly sat at her table, soaking up every tidbit, no doubt. Unlike the others, Karly had taken off her mask.

Leah reached up and took off her mask, dropping it to

the table and then sat down. "I thought they were required," she said, determined to brazen the whole awkward situation out.

"Oh, they are, but we can't expect bad girl Leah Camacho to pay attention to that," Karly said with an indulgent smile as if they were old friends. "So I was right, you and Drew are more than just fuck buddies! Does this mean you're moving to Fort Worth with him when he takes the new job?"

"Fort Worth?" she asked, her voice sounding strained even to her own ears.

Leah froze in her seat. Fort Worth? In all the hours they'd spent talking last night, he'd never mentioned a new job once. In fact, he'd been open to coming up to Denver to see if he'd like it. Wait. Had he said that? Specifically? Fingernails digging into the palms of her hand, she tried to recall his exact words and realized he'd evaded giving a direct answer. She'd just filled in the blanks with what she wanted to believe. Just like she had that summer when he'd left her without a goodbye.

"Oh yeah. From what I hear, this week was just one last hurrah in Catfish Creek before he starts with the Fort Worth Police Department next week. It was totally good luck that you were here to take advantage of the moment," Karly said. "I guess you two will always have Catfish Creek though."

No. They wouldn't. Not anymore. History had repeated itself one too many times.

Without uttering another word to Karly, Leah shoved her chair back from the table and marched away, her only objective being to get the hell out of Catfish Creek. She never should have come back.

"Leah," Drew grabbed her arm as she passed by the bar, jerking her to a stop, "everything okay?"

"Just fine and dandy," she managed to get out between clenched teeth. "Congrats on the job. Good luck in Fort Worth."

Confusion formed a deep V between his eyes. "What are you talking about—"

"Don't bother." She yanked her arm free, missing the warmth of his touch as much as she hated herself for being weak enough to still want it. "Karly told me everything about your new job and how you're starting on Monday. Wow, it really is like deja vu all over again with us, isn't it."

"That's not how it is." He held up his hands, palms forward, the panicked look in his eyes telling her everything she needed to know.

This is what Catfish Creek did to people. It made them do stupid shit over and over and over again until all that was left of them was a half crazy shell. Drew claimed that he'd been stuck in a cycle when really it was her, falling deeper and deeper in love with the same man who only broke her heart every damn time. It was ridiculous and she'd had more than enough.

"Of course it is. But don't worry. You won't be the one to leave without a word this time," she said, furiously blinking back the tears making her vision swim. "I'm already gone."

And she was. She swerved around him and hustled toward the doors so focused on making her escape that she didn't even see anyone else there until she ran smack dab into her and nearly knocked the other woman off her feet. They bobbled for a second before the woman locked one hand around Leah's arm, steadying herself. It took a second but the woman's name clicked into place. Rae. They'd had chemistry together and had been friendly, if not friends—especially when it came to the assholery of male nerds who thought a couple of chicks had invaded their space.

"Oh, my God, Leah, I'm so sorry," Rea wheezed, her free hand clutched to her chest as she regained her footing.

"Don't be sorry. I'm not mad at you." No, all her anger was aimed at only one person—herself. Once again she'd fallen for Drew Jackson.

Fury beating her insides to a pulp, she yanked open the door and strode out of the school, holding her head high even as she dragged her bloodied, mutilated heart in her wake.

∼

Drew

Brain knocked off-line, he stood like an asshole and watched as she stormed out of the gym. He had no fucking idea what had just happened. How in the hell... Karly sidled up next to him, a fake smile turning her lips and an assessing look in her shit-stirring eyes.

"Oh my gosh," she said with a simper. "I didn't cause any trouble, did I?"

"Trouble?" His brain started to rev back into gear. "You? No. You're annoying, a pest, a gossip with nothing better to do but hiss snide comments about other people's lives. Trouble is that woman who just walked out the door and it's the kind I can't live without."

Leaving an open-mouthed Karly in his rearview, he hustled out of the gym determined not to lose Leah when he'd been lucky enough to get a second chance with her. She was in the parking lot by the time he caught up with her. How she managed to be that fast in heels, he had no damn clue.

"Leah," he called out.

She kept going, only the slight falter in her step gave him any sense that she'd heard him. Heart hammering against his chest like it was gonna crack right through his ribs, he sprinted to her. The urge to reach out and physically tie her to him so she couldn't run almost brought him to his knees. He couldn't though. He made one move toward her and like a cornered coyote, she'd charge and aim right for his balls.

"Dammit, Leah." He shoved his hands in his pockets as he kept pace with her breakneck pace. "Stop. I'm not going to Fort Worth."

"It doesn't matter," she said with just enough wobble in her voice to turn his stomach inside out. "It's not like any of this mattered outside of the strange bubble of Catfish Creek."

"Bullshit." Desperate to get her to understand he wasn't the boy he was that summer anymore, he was the man who wanted to spend the rest of his life with her, he sped up and pivoted into her path, blocking her getaway. "Do you know what I did when I left you all snug in my bed last night?"

She didn't answer, but she didn't move either. It wasn't much but it was probably the best sign of encouragement he was going to get from her at this moment.

"I emailed the Fort Worth Police Department and withdrew my application. Then, I spent the next few hours applying for a job at every police department I could find within an hour of Denver," he said. "After that, I bought a pair of snow boots and a real life winter jacket because no matter what happens with the job—hell, I'll take a night shift security guard position—I need to be near you."

Ever the hard ass, Leah arched an eyebrow and crossed her arms in front of her body. "You lied to me. Maybe not outright, but by omission and I'm done making the same mistake over and over again. What do you want, for me to start a slow clap because of your bravery in deciding to leave Texas?"

"No, I want you to realize what you mean to me, what you've always meant to me, but I was too fucking dumb to figure it out any faster than this. I love you, Leah Camacho." She didn't move, didn't flinch in the slightest at his declaration. He sucked in as much of a steadying breath as he could, determined not to stop until he'd confessed it all. "I love that you make me nuts. I love that you wear your bad girl attitude like armor. I love that underneath all that black you wear nothing but hot pink lace. I love that you always keep me guessing. I love that you are the best kind of trouble there is." The hard expression on her beautiful face made him hurt. Fuck that. Agony was squeezing his chest hard enough to make him want to double over and cry for mercy, but he kept going. "I know you want to run. It's written all over your face. Don't do it. Or better yet, let me run beside you. I know exactly why my life has been on a loop until now, because it was leading me to you. No matter what I did, where I went, or how much I fought it, my life was *always* leading me back to you. Together we work. I don't know why. We just do and I'm sorr--"

Leah pressed a finger to his mouth, stopping him midsentence. His heart sputtered to a stop as the words died on his tongue. This was it. He could see a decision in her eyes. He'd either convinced her or he was going to have to continue this grovel in Denver.

"I know why," she said, a soft smile curling up one side of her mouth. "I've probably known somewhere deep down since I was six years old, but it seems like I was just as slow as you were." Her finger brushed across his lips and he couldn't stop himself from kissing the tip. "We work because we're different sides of the same coin."

It made sense. He was always Mr. Law and Order and she was little Miss Trouble. "Head and tails."

"Yeah." She took a step closer, eliminating every inch of space separating them.

His hands seemed to move of their own accord, automatically going to her because he couldn't ever seem to stop touching her. "You do have a phenomenal ass."

Leah threw back her head and laughed. "Really? That's what you're going with at a time like this?"

He dipped his head lower. "I never said I had your brains."

She tilted her chin just the right amount to bring her lips within millimeters of his. "But you do have my heart."

"And you've got mine, Sweets." He claimed her lush mouth, not only for tonight but for tomorrow and every trouble-filled tomorrow after that.

Isaac

Nothing tasted like home quite as much as a breakfast burger from The Hamburger Shack. It was a half a pound of hamburger wrapped in bacon, topped with an egg and square of crispy hash browns and sandwiched between two thick slabs of Texas toast. His mouth was salivating as soon as the waitress dropped off his plate. Tamara looked doubtful.

"You're going to have a heart attack before we even get back to Fort Worth," she said, shaking her head.

"Totally worth it." He reached out to double fist it, but his phone buzzed on the table.

MARKO: Everything OK with ur sis?

ISAAC: Y

MARKO: Then get ur ass back here. New assignment.

He glanced down at the breakfast burger, already regretting leaving his phone on.

ISAAC: Why don't you take it?

MARKO: Working on something with Elisa.

ISAAC: Besides striking out with her?

MARKO: Ur so ducking funny.

He snorted.

ISAAC: Ducking? Maybe your clumsy fingers are the problem. I can give tips. Do you require guidance?

MARKO: 👍

ISAAC: Emojis? You're so cute. What's next, a sparkly unicorn tattoo?

MARKO: Fuck off and get back here.

Tamara was already halfway through whatever horrible and healthy thing she'd managed to find at The Hamburger Shack. His burger was still untouched. What a sin.

ISAAC: Right after breakfast.

MARKO: Eat in the car.

Isaac snapped a picture of the burger and hit send.

MARKO: Carry on and grab me one of those to go.

ISAAC: Only if you say pretty please.

MARKO: 👍

Isaac laughed and set his phone down before flagging the waitress.

"Everything okay?" Tamara asked, her tone was light but he could see the fierceness just below her icy exterior.

That was his girl, ready to do battle for those she considered hers. God, he loved her. And if he kept his foot hard on the gas on the rental since the helicopter was in use by other B-Squad members, he could probably get her back to Fort Worth, naked and satisfied, before anyone else on the team knew they'd gotten home. Anytime spent between her sweet thighs was always the best part of his day and was definitely worth the speeding ticket.

"Yeah, new assignment."

"What's the B-Squad up to next?" Tamara asked, excitement sparking in her blue eyes.

"Got me." Isaac shrugged and picked up his breakfast burger. "But I bet it'll be fun as hell."

Bad Boy Homecoming

Thank you so much for reading Trouble, I hope you loved Drew and Leah as much as I did. And if you're curious about the B-Squad, check out the entire series.

Drew and Leah's story is part of the fun and sexy Bad Boy Homecoming series. Each book is a complete stand alone but we hope you'll go through each of the romances to see your favorite characters make special appearances and see just how the reunion went down. Each book carries at least one of our favorite tropes as well as a few high school flashbacks that make us smile and shake our heads. If you enjoyed the book, we'd love if you could please leave a review to show us how much. Reviews help authors every day and we totally appreciate it.

THANK you for coming to the Bad Boy Homecoming reunion and we hope you'll not only find a romance you love, but a few authors as well.

xoxo, Avery

The Books of Bad Boy Homecoming

Dropout by Carrie Ann Ryan
Trouble by Avery Flynn
Prom Queen by Katee Robert
Honor by Kennedy Layne
Rock Star Stacey Kennedy

Want more Bad Boy Homecoming? Read on to check out the next romance in our sexy reunion stand alone series: Prom Queen by Katee Robert

THE B-SQUAD SERIES

Bulletproof: A MacKenzie/B-Squad Book 0.5

From Liliana Hart's New York Times bestselling MacKenzie family comes a new story by best-selling author Avery Flynn...

"Being one of the good guys is not my thing."

Bianca Sutherland isn't at an exclusive Eyes-Wide-Shut style orgy for the orgasms. She's there because the only clue to her friend's disappearance is a photo of a painting hanging somewhere in Bisu Manor. Determined to find her missing friend when no one else will, she expects trouble when she cons her way into the party—but not in the form of a so-hot-he-turns-your-panties-to-ash former boxer.

Taz Hazard's only concern is looking out for himself and he has no intention of changing his ways until he finds sexy-as-sin Bianca at the most notorious mansion in Ft. Worth.

Now, he's tangled up in a missing person case tied into a powerful new drug about to flood the streets, if they can't find a way to stop it before its too late. Taking on a drug cartel isn't safe, but when passion ignites between them Taz and Bianca discover their hearts aren't bulletproof either.

Get Your Copy Today!

Brazen: B-Squad Book One

Falling in love is the easy part, staying together...now that's the biggest challenge of all.

Everything is finally working out for Bianca Sutherland and Taz Hazard. They're in love and running B-Squad Security and Investigations. They've planned the perfect operation to take down the dangerous drug kingpin who's kidnapped one of Bianca's best friends. Easy as right? Then Taz's wife—who was supposed to be his ex-wife—shows up on the eve of the big rescue mission and threatens to blow up his and Bianca's happily ever after. Can you say awkward?

The last thing Bianca wants after the revelation that Taz might still be married, MARRIED!! is to have to spend time with her very recently former live-in boyfriend who never told her he'd ever been married in the first place, ugh. But it's too late to change plans now. To save her friend, she has to put on her big girl panties and go undercover with Taz as a newlywed couple at an exclusive resort.

The only thing Taz wants is Bianca and he's willing to do whatever it takes to win her back. But when it's his life on the line, will it be too late for him to show her that his past is over and she's the only woman for his future or will he lose her forever?

Brazen is a stand alone novel and the first full novel in the B-Squad series. However, if you need to find out how Taz and Bianca met and fell in love, check out Bulletproof, a novella set in Liliana Hart's MacKenzie Security world.

Get Your Copy Today!

Bang: B-Squad Book Two

Freelance investigator Isaac Camacho has a weakness for hot bitchy blondes, and no one fits the bill quite like former beauty queen and gold digger Tamara Post. She's sexy, feisty and on the run from a tyrannical cult leader. Isaac is like a walking magnet for complicated women. He loves them almost as much as he loves watching Tamara act like a total ice queen when he knows she burns white hot.

Calculating opportunist Tamara Post never cared what anyone thought about her—except for her sister. But when her sister dies, it's up to Tamara to hide her teenage niece so the girl's dictatorial father can't marry her off to one of his way too old for her disciples. The last thing Tamara has time for is Isaac—a man who flirts as well as he fills out a pair of worn jeans and does so as easy as breathing and whose stubborn determination to help makes it hard to act as if she's really as cold as she appears. Why is it that he's the only one who sees the real her?

When the bad guys find her, there's only one-person Tamara can depend on to help keep her alive until her niece is safe. But once the life and death chase is on, it's not just their lives Tamara and Isaac are risking...but their hearts.

Hold onto your heart with this story, sometimes the person below the surface really is worth fighting for.

Get Your Copy Today!

Blade: A B-Squad Novella

Bad girl Gillie Pike has gone straight, finally, but someone with a lot of money wants to bring her out of retirement to steal the Cup and make sure it's found in star goalie Flynn Kazakov's possession. But there's got to be a catch right? It can't be as easy as that.

They call him Crazy-kov for a reason and nothing makes him more nuts than his best friend's sexy little sister who swears she's the only one who can keep him out of jail and on the ice.

But what happens when they start to heat up the ice? Can they beat the buzzer and outwit the bad guys or will it be game over for them both?

Get Your Copy Today!

Trouble: A B-Squad Novella

A high school reunion is about to get down and dirty and a whole lot more complicated in this new romance from USA Today bestselling author Avery Flynn.

Brains and a badass attitude. That's all troublemaker Leah Camacho took with her when she left Catfish Creek as fast as she could. She'd promised herself she'd never go

back, NEVER. But when the invite to her tenth high school reunion arrived along with the chance to show everyone who doubted her what a success she's made of herself and okay to rub their noses in her success, she couldn't resist. However, when she discovers a 15-carat, stolen diamond in her rental car's glove box, there's only one man she can turn to for help—the same undeniably sexy, stubborn domineering man who'd smashed her heart all those years ago.

Sheriff Drew Jackson knew a long time ago that Leah Camacho was nothing but trouble in a sexy as sin package and has sworn to never get caught up in her again—no matter how damn hot she is or how badly he'd failed to forget her. But, when the woman who once test drove his heart right into a concrete wall rolls into Catfish Creek with some serious bad guys on her tail, it's up to him to keep her safe—even if that means guarding her hot bod 24/7 without giving into temptation or losing his mind.

But can the past be re-written to make this the happy ending they both deserve or are they headed for heartbreak once again?

Get Your Copy Today!

ABOUT AVERY FLYNN

USA Today Bestselling romance author Avery Flynn has three slightly-wild children, loves a hockey-addicted husband and is desperately hoping someone invents the coffee IV drip.

She was a reader before she was a writer and hopes to always be both. She loves to write about smartass alpha heroes who are as good with a quip as they are with their *ahem* other God-given talents. Her heroines are feisty, fierce and fantastic. Brainy and brave, these ladies know how to stand on their own two feet and knock the bad guys off theirs.

Find out more about Avery on her **website**, follow her on **Twitter** and **Pinterest**, like her on her **Facebook page** or friend her on her **Facebook profile**. She's also on **Goodreads** and **BookLikes**.

Join her street team, The Flynnbots, and receive special sneak peeks, prizes and early access to her latest releases!

Also, if you figure out how to send Oreos through the Internet, she'll be your best friend for life.

Contact her at avery@averyflynn.com. She'd love to hear from you!

ALSO BY AVERY FLYNN

The B-Squad Series

Bulletproof

Brazen (B-Squad 1)

Bang (B-Squad 2)

Blade (B-Squad 2.5)

Trouble (B-Squad 2.75 & Bad Boy Homecoming)

Harbor City Romance Series

The Negotiator

The Killer Style Series

High-Heeled Wonder (Killer Style 1)

This Year's Black (Killer Style 2)

Make Me Up (Killer Style 3)

Designed For Murder (Killer Style 4)

The Laytons Series

Dangerous Kiss (Laytons 1)

Dangerous Flirt (Laytons 2)

Dangerous Tease (Laytons 3)

The Dangerous Love Bundle: The Entire Laytons Series

The Retreat Series

Dodging Temptation (The Retreat Book 1)

The Sweet Salvation Brewery Series

Enemies on Tap (Sweet Salvation Brewery 1)

Hollywood on Tap (Sweet Salvation Brewery 2)

PROM QUEEN BY KATEE ROBERT

"I can't do it. I won't." Jessica Jackson backed around the kitchen table, feeling like seven different kinds of a fool when Brooklyn Jameson followed her, waving the invitation that had caused all of this. "Stop it. You're being ridiculous."

"No, you're being ridiculous." Brooklyn lunged.

Jessica scrambled back, nearly taking out a chair as she did. The open and airy kitchen felt too small for the first time in the five years she'd lived here. "I'm not going. End of story." She edged around the corner of the island, not liking the way her friend eyed the counter like it was an obstacle to be overcome.

"Bullshit. It'd be one thing if you were like me, who barely went to high school enough to pass. Or Cora, with her fancy private tutors."

"I can hear you." Cora Lander's voice floated down from her room upstairs.

Brooklyn shot a look at the open balcony and then refocused on Jessica. "You have to go." She raised her voice. "Cora, tell her she has to go."

"You have to go."

Jessica glared and slid back a step, eyeing the French doors that led out to the beach. It would be a perfect escape—if Brooklyn wasn't standing in the way. "What is this? Why do you care so much if I go to some stupid reunion or not?"

"Oh please." Brooklyn huffed. "I'm a private detective, remember? Even if I wasn't, I could detect that you want to go to this damn reunion by the longing looks you've been sending this invitation ever since it showed up in February—four freaking months ago. Just suck it up and go."

She wanted to, but only because she apparently has a masochistic streak a mile wide. Jessica stopped trying to flee and threw her hands up. "You don't get it. I was a bitch in high school—no, I was the queen bitch. I was so terrible to some of those people. How am I supposed to face them knowing some of the crap I pulled?"

Brooklyn snorted and cocked her head to the side, sending her fall of auburn hair cascading over one shoulder. It was the only part of her that was girlish to the extreme. The rest of her was dressed in layers designed to make people look right through her—even in the heat of Los Angeles's summer. She rolled her eyes. "It was high school. Everyone was a little shit in high school."

"Not like me." Jessica had taken mean girl to a whole new level. She'd been so sure of her place and life—and that she ranked above everyone else. Since the catastrophe that was graduation, she'd more than balanced her karmic debt. She hoped. If there was anything left to pay, going back to face her former victims would do it. "Please don't make me go."

Brooklyn narrowed her amber eyes. "This isn't about you being a dick. This is about him."

"No, it's not." She spoke too quickly and then mentally cursed herself for giving away the truth.

Not that her friends were unaware of her history with Jake Davis. She'd met Cora in her third year in LA, and Brooklyn a couple months later. They'd lived together for five years. These women had seen The Breakdown of 2012, when she'd hit rock bottom so spectacularly that she'd plowed right through it to a whole new low. She'd lost the only acting job she'd been able score in five long years, lost her sorta-boyfriend, and lost her apartment in the space of a week. It was in the midst of that that she'd gotten the drunkest she'd ever been in her entire life and confessed everything.

About how she'd been so crazy in love with Jake the entire time they'd dated in high school. How they'd been each other's firsts. How they'd planned a perfect future together.

And how she'd dumped him on his ass the first hiccup they had, because she was sure he was going to hold her back from her destiny.

Jessica snorted. Destiny. She'd been a little twat. Knowing that now didn't mean she was eager to face the one who got away. More like the one I kicked to the curb.

"Oh, good Lord, you have that moony look in your eyes." Brooklyn made a gagging sound. "Cora, come talk some sense into her!"

Footsteps padded upstairs and then Cora's head appeared over the balcony. Her dark eyes took in their positions—Jessica still wanting to flee and Brooklyn standing in her way—and huffed out a breath. "You're going, end of story. If it will make you feel better, you can pretend I forced you."

Considering Cora could be downright scary when she wanted to be, there was some truth to the statement.

Jessica wasn't backing down this time. "You don't get it."

"Wrong. Out of all of us, I know all about having to face down your past on a daily basis. I manage. You will, too."

Okay, maybe you do get it. Jessica gritted her teeth. It didn't matter. It was apples and oranges. "Y'all cannot seriously expect me to go face the firing squad. I'm willing to eat my humble pie when the situation calls for it, but this is just too much. I don't have anything resembling a boyfriend. I am almost thirty years old and have two roommates. I haven't accomplished jack all that I said I would when I blew out of town with two middle fingers in the air."

Cora smiled, her teeth perfectly white and straight against her blood red lips. "I thought your therapist said facing down your past was an important part of your journey."

"I have faced down my past. I'm reformed. That doesn't mean I want to be thrown to the wolves so I can play a damn martyr."

Brooklyn laughed, her long brown hair swinging in its ponytail. "A martyr. You have such an inflated opinion of yourself."

"Shut it." She turned a pleading look at Cora. "Let's just pretend this never happened, okay?"

Cora's expression turned contemplative. "You know what your problem is? It isn't going back to Catfish Creek. It's going back alone."

Something like hope blossomed in Jessica's chest. She'd seen both her parents and her brother quite a few times over the last ten years, but she'd never been brave enough to cross the town lines. Though she was mostly too proud—

even now—to admit it, she missed at least some parts of Catfish Creek. "You have an idea."

"I have a brilliant idea. Come on."

Jessica headed for the stairs, Brooklyn hot on her heels. She found Cora back in her bedroom at the desk she'd set up for when she needed to work from home. It was just as light and airy as the rest of the house, the big windows overlooking the beach giving the space plenty of natural light, and the seafoam green walls and white furniture gave the space a restful feeling.

Though Jessica wasn't feeling particularly restful at the moment. One look at Cora's laptop had her shaking her head. "No way."

"One of my clients used the company, and they're perfectly respectable." Cora scrolled down, giving them an eyeful of the classy website that offered all manner of dates. Jessica caught sight of one package that included having a beautiful man show up to a residence and clean for the allotted time.

"You have got to be kidding me. Escorts?"

"That's illegal in both California and Texas. No, the sex isn't included—it's strictly forbidden. You can't even kiss them." Cora touched the screen. "There we go. This is the package Hilary went with. She had a wedding and didn't feel like dealing with people gossiping about her cheating ex-husband, so she took a date. He charmed everyone and kept them distracted from unfortunate lines of questions, which freed her up to have a good time. That's exactly what you need."

It sounded too good to be true. Jessica leaned forward, scanning the package Cora had brought up. She would put in her information and her basic requests—everything from looks to background—and once it was all agreed upon, her date would meet her locally and play his role for the duration of the trip. They limited these to three days, but she wouldn't need much more than that. Get in, attend the reunion, get out.

Then she noticed the price. "Oh, hell, no. I can't afford that!"

Cora rotated her chair around and considered her with unblinking dark eyes. "You need this, Jess. You need to go face him—and everyone else—so you can actually move on. All the therapy and self-help books in the world won't mean a damn thing if you can't take this step."

Jake. It all came back to Jake.

The rest of her graduating class weren't terrible people or anything, but she didn't feel the loss over not being in contact with them. Jake was just this gaping hole in her chest. Oh, it had scabbed over in the years since she'd seen him, but the boyfriends she'd had since then couldn't hold a candle against the phantom of Jake.

She'd never be able to have a lasting relationship if she didn't put him firmly in the past where he belonged, and she couldn't do that until they have a very painful and much-needed conversation.

For me, at least. He's moved on with his life.

One night a couple years ago, driven by Brooklyn egging her on and just enough tequila to drown out common sense, she'd searched him out on Facebook. His profile was only half private, so she was able to see a few pictures of him, but nothing else. He had looked even better at twenty-six than he had at eighteen, and that he still had his annual fishing trip with the boys, but she had no idea if he was married or had kids.

The thought made her sick to her stomach.

She pressed a hand there, as if the pain was a physical thing she could combat. "I don't know."

"Too late."

Jessica spun to face Brooklyn so fast, she almost fell on her ass. "What did you say?"

Her friend didn't look up from her phone. "You're booked. It's paid for. You can assist me on a couple stakeouts to pay me back."

She grabbed the phone from Brooklyn's hand and read with dawning horror. All American guy, blond, painfully hot. Needs to be able to deal with the fact that I was a bitch in high school and so most of these people are going to hate me and be dicks. "Are you kidding me?"

"What? It's the truth." Brooklyn snatched the phone back. "You can thank me later."

Jessica stood there as the truth came crashing down around her. She was going back to Catfish Creek. She could cancel the date, but it wouldn't change anything because Cora and Brooklyn were right—she needed to face her past. Her hand itched with the need to call her therapist or pop a Xanax, but she resisted both urges. She'd been using crutches for far too long. Maybe it was time for her to do what was necessary to finally move on.

She just hoped it wouldn't kill her in the process.

JAKE DAVIS STARED at the computer, wondering if he was hallucinating. That would explain seeing goddamn Jessica fucking Jackson's name on the newest batch of requests for Diamond Dates. He sat back and took a long drink of his coffee, but nothing changed.

She was coming back for the reunion.

More than that, she was obviously single if she was looking for a fake date to bring with her.

Of course she was. If she was single, she wouldn't want to face Catfish Creek—face him—alone.

Jake couldn't begin to count the number of times he'd shown up for events around town since high school and been party to pitying looks and barely concealed whispers. Nothing people loved more than a good scandal, and his ex was nothing if not a good scandal.

It was when he ran into Rae Evans that things started to come together. They'd both been invited to one of their graduating class's wedding, and agreed to go together just to avoid dealing with the nonsense.

It worked.

No one bothered them. There were looks, of course, but neither of them had to answer any uncomfortable questions about being single—or what their exes were up to.

And so Diamond Dates was born.

He sat back in his chair and looked around, trying to get some distance on this. His office was exactly the same as it had been since the day he moved the company here—dark gray walls, a generic sofa that could double as a bed in a pinch, and a single window overlooking the street. It wasn't fancy, but he didn't need fancy. Diamond Dates didn't meet its clients face to face. They handled everything online or over the phone. In the event that a meeting was required, he set it up in a public place.

In the years since he'd started the company, he'd only had to deal with one over-zealous client, but one was more than enough. His guys trusted him to keep their personal information locked down and to keep things professional. The best way to do that was to confine the entire encounter to whatever event they were contracted for.

None of that made a damn bit of difference when it came to Jessica Jackson. There would be no distance for him. Even trying for it was fucking impossible.

If he was a petty asshole, he could use this application to humiliate the hell out of her. They might have graduated ten years ago, but there were still people walking around Catfish Creek with emotional scars from shit she'd pulled back in the day. They'd be like sharks scenting blood in the water, glorying in seeing her brought to her knees with them standing witness.

He stopped and really thought about it. What was the point? Hurting her now wouldn't take them back in time and erase the pain he'd felt. Would he like to see her with some egg on her face? Sure. He wasn't a damn saint. But that didn't mean he could be the one to pull the trigger.

She might have ripped his still-beating heart of out of his chest and ground it beneath one of her spike heels, but she'd been his first love. Fuck, she'd been his only love— being burned so spectacularly created a whole hell of a lot of trust issues, and he hadn't bothered to get past most of them.

Fuck, I'm depressing.

He brought up the information that Jessica had sent in. Jake did background checks on all his potential clients. Just because the majority of them were women didn't mean his guys were safe. It paid to be safe and to have his shit together before sending them out.

He'd thought about checking up on her over the years, but Jake had never crossed that line. She was his ex for a reason, and she'd made it abundantly clear that she was better off without him after the injury that killed all his college and NFL plans. It had been hard enough recovering while dealing with a broken heart. He didn't need to get kicked in the teeth of his own volition.

Now, he was practically required to look her up.

Jake plugged her information into his program and then pulled up the photo she'd sent while it worked on the search. He set his coffee on the desk so he didn't spill it on himself. She looks good. Better than good. The Jessica he knew had been all angles as harsh and unforgiving as the personality she showed the world. Whoever had taken this picture had captured the softer side of her that she'd only ever shown Jake...right up until she didn't.

She was half turned toward the camera, the sun behind her left shoulder and giving her dark hair an angelic cast as it tangled around her head in a breeze he could almost feel. With the ocean at her back and the half smile on her face, she looked...happy. She'd been hotter than hell as a blond. With her natural dark hair, she was downright stunning.

He spent one useless minute wondering if a boyfriend had taken the picture before Jake made himself set it aside. He should reject her request. She obviously didn't know that he owned Diamond Dates or she wouldn't have tried to use it to book a date. If she realized, she'd be humiliated, even if he was the only person who knew it happened.

While he considered his options, he scanned the info the search had brought up. A few unpaid parking tickets, an address that was right on the beach, and a job she'd worked at for five years. An insurance company. He pulled up a new tab and Googled the name, and then huffed out a laugh. He hadn't realized that a person could insure their individual body parts. "Only in LA."

What the fuck was he going to do about this?

Even as the thought crossed his mind, a plan formed. Jake shook his head, a rueful grin taking root. Apparently he wasn't as above petty revenge as he'd thought. He wouldn't reject Jessica's bid. He wouldn't be sending one of his guys to meet her, either. Even after all this time, Jake couldn't stand the thought of seeing her with someone else, even knowing it'd be fake.

No, he'd be the one waiting for Jessica when she got off that plane.

And then?

Well, then they'd see how things fell out.

GET YOUR COPY TODAY:

The Books of Bad Boy Homecoming

Dropout by Carrie Ann Ryan
Trouble by Avery Flynn
Prom Queen by Katee Robert
Honor by Kennedy Layne
Rock Star Stacey Kennedy

29392744R00104

Made in the USA
Middletown, DE
22 December 2018